Jim Benton's Tales from Mackerel Middle School

OUR DUMB DIARY

SCHOLASTIC INC.

New York   Toronto   London   Auckland   Sydney

Mexico City   New Delhi   Hong Kong   Buenos Aires

We dedicate this book to:

_____

_____

_____

_____

Thanks to Maria Barbo, who worked from afar, and
Shannon Penney, who did her work from aclose.

Thanks also to Steve Scott, Kay Petronio,
Susan Jeffers Casel, and Craig Walker.

ISBN-13: 978-0-545-16683-6
ISBN-10: 0-545-16683-7
Copyright ©2006 by Jim Benton

12 11 10 9 8 7 6 5 4 3   9 10 11 12 13 14/0

Printed in China
This edition first printing, September 2009

WARNING

GREAT DANGER AWAITS
YE WHO READS FURTHER.

The
Last
Person
Who
Kept
Reading →

seriously,
you have a bowl of
TUNA Casserole where your
soul is supposed to Be
if you read a person's
Diary

I'm serious. Thou shalt be **CURSED** if thou READS FURTHER. AND you can tell I'm serious because it says <u>SHALT</u> AND <u>thou</u>.

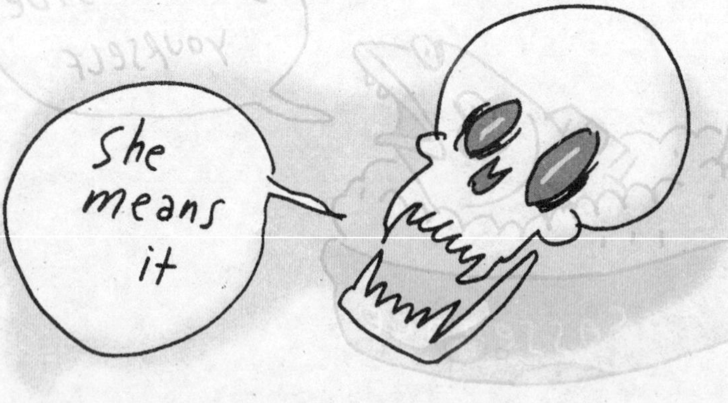
She means it

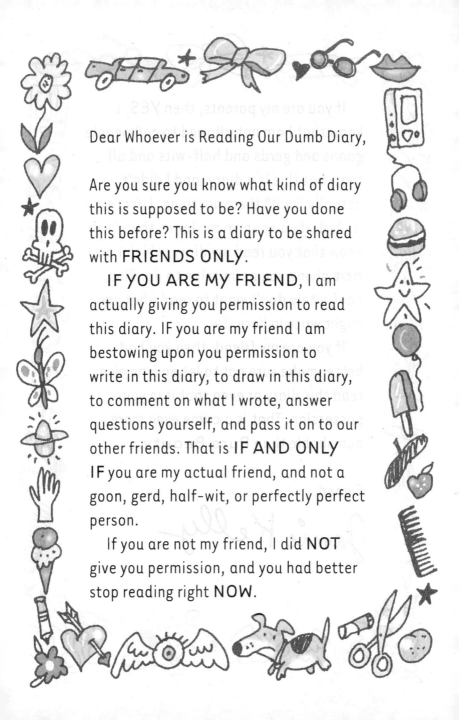

Dear Whoever is Reading Our Dumb Diary,

Are you sure you know what kind of diary this is supposed to be? Have you done this before? This is a diary to be shared with **FRIENDS ONLY**.

IF YOU ARE MY FRIEND, I am actually giving you permission to read this diary. IF you are my friend I am bestowing upon you permission to write in this diary, to draw in this diary, to comment on what I wrote, answer questions yourself, and pass it on to our other friends. That is **IF AND ONLY IF** you are my actual friend, and not a goon, gerd, half-wit, or perfectly perfect person.

If you are not my friend, I did **NOT** give you permission, and you had better stop reading right **NOW**.

If you are my parents, then YES, I know that I am not allowed to call people goons and gerds and half-wits and all that, but this is a diary, and I didn't actually "call" them anything. I wrote it. And, if you punish me for it, then I will know that you read my diary, which I am **not** giving you permission to do. Plus, I definitely don't want to read what you might write in here. Ew.

If you are my friend, then you had better make sure not to let anyone else read this diary or even spot it in your possession. That is a crime even more punishable than **Pure Beauty**.

Signed,

Jamie Kelly

See? I'm not kidding about this.

By the power vested in me, I, _____,
(YOUR NAME HERE)
do promise that everything in this diary is true, or at
least as true as I think it needs to be. I also promise not
to show Our Dumb Diary to anyone who has not signed
an oath of secrecy, or who qualifies as a turd.

By the power vested in me, I, _____,
(YOUR NAME HERE)
do promise that everything in this diary is true, or at
least as true as I think it needs to be. I also promise not
to show Our Dumb Diary to anyone who has not signed
an oath of secrecy, or who qualifies as a turd.

By the power vested in me, I, _____,
(YOUR NAME HERE)
do promise that everything in this diary is true, or at
least as true as I think it needs to be. I also promise not
to show Our Dumb Diary to anyone who has not signed
an oath of secrecy, or who qualifies as a turd.

By the power vested in me, I, _____,
(YOUR NAME HERE)
do promise that everything in this diary is true, or at
least as true as I think it needs to be. I also promise not
to show Our Dumb Diary to anyone who has not signed
an oath of secrecy, or who qualifies as a turd.

THIS DIARY IS BEING SHARED BY...

NAME:

NICKNAME:

SCHOOL:

LOCKER:

PET:

EYE COLOR:

HAIR COLOR:

OCCUPATION:

DESTINY:

NAME:

NICKNAME:

SCHOOL:

LOCKER:

PET:

EYE COLOR:

HAIR COLOR:

OCCUPATION:

DESTINY:

NAME:

NICKNAME:

SCHOOL:

LOCKER:

PET:

EYE COLOR:

HAIR COLOR:

OCCUPATION:

DESTINY:

NAME:

NICKNAME:

SCHOOL:

LOCKER:

PET:

EYE COLOR:

HAIR COLOR:

OCCUPATION:

DESTINY:

Protect your Dumb Diary from vengeful beagles, nosy parents, sneaky siblings, and dimwits!

"Angeline was all excited when she found out that I keep a diary, because she says that she does, too.

But then she asked if she could read it.

Awkward, right? Since on one or two occasions, I may have written something unpleasant about Angeline . . ."

Jamie Kelly

What would you do if someone asked to read this book?

OUR IDEAS:

_____

_____

_____

_____

Like at First Sight

"Dumb Diary, did I ever tell you how Isabella and I became friends? It was instantaneous. It's what people call **Like at First Sight**. It was way back in second grade. On the first day of school, our teacher, Miss Baker, was asking us all to stand up and say our names. Isabella stood and said, "I'm Isabella Vinchella," and Lewis Clarke giggled.

It took three teachers and half the class to pull Isabella off Lewis, who she seemed to be playing like a fat little xylophone. (He actually made higher notes when she punched him in certain places.) Violence is never the answer, of course, unless your question is "Hey Isabella, what's the answer?" But I admired the fact that she was like some sort of dangerous little mousetrap that you just should not stick your fingers in. I told her so, and she liked the description.

We became instant friends, and have been that way ever since — although sometimes Isabella seems less like a mousetrap and more like an atomic bomb that you should not stick your fingers in."

Jamie Kelly

What was your first impression of your best friend? Was it like at first sight . . . or not?

Write the story of you and your BFF here!

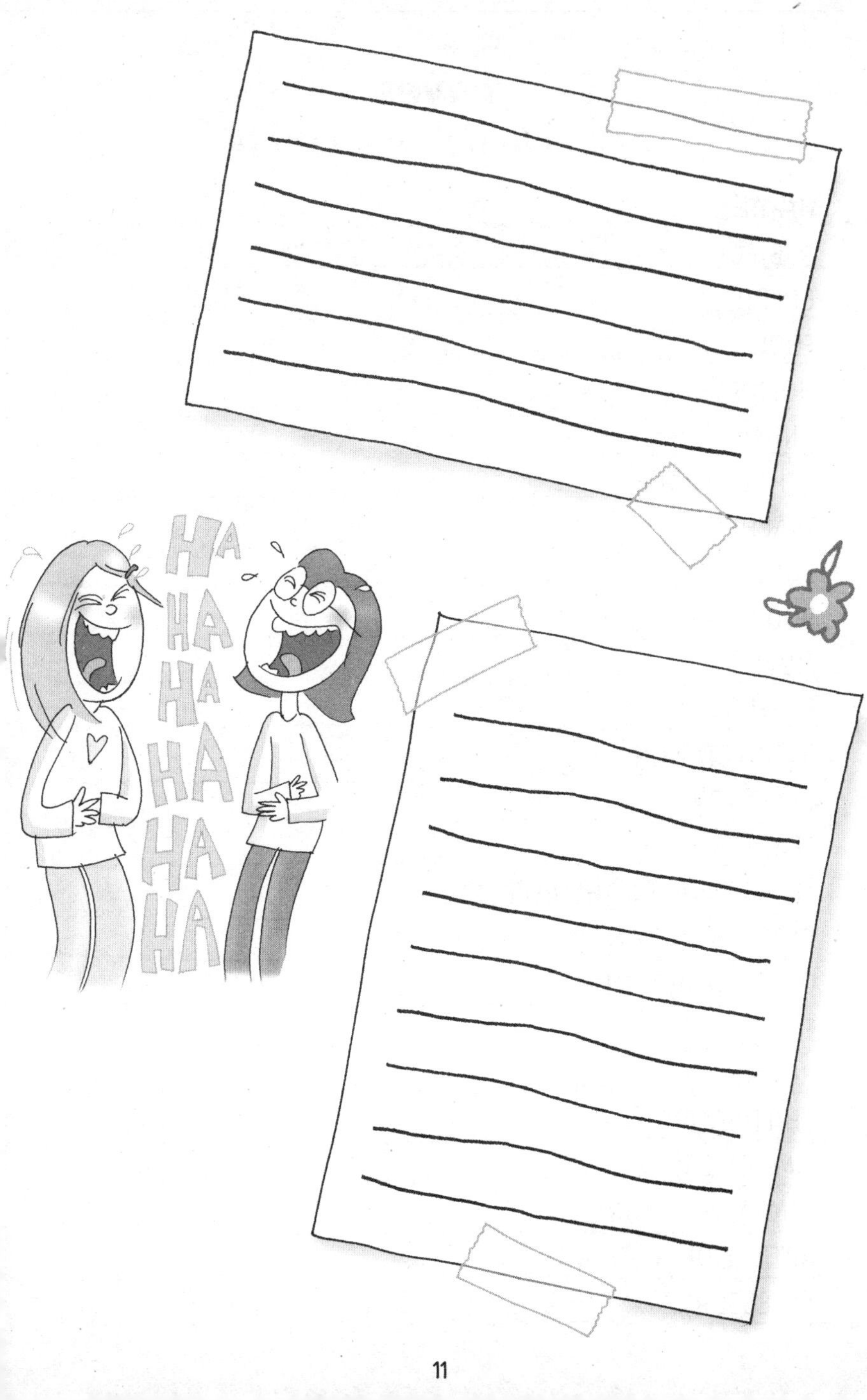
HA
HA
HA
HA
HA
HA

Faves
or: Things I Don't Hate

NAME:

SUBJECT:

COLOR:

FOOD:

HOLIDAY:

ANIMAL:

SCHOOL LUNCH:

TEACHER:

SONG:

BOOK:

MOVIE:

TV SHOW:

RADIO STATION:

CELEBRITY:

FEATURE:

THING TO DO ON THE WEEKEND:

STORE IN THE MALL:

OUTDOOR ACTIVITY:

FAMILY MEMBER:

ROOM IN MY HOUSE:

CHILDHOOD TOY:

TIME OF DAY:

FAMILY VACATION:

ARTICLE OF CLOTHING:

ACCESSORY:

NAME:

SUBJECT:

COLOR:

FOOD:

HOLIDAY:

ANIMAL:

SCHOOL LUNCH:

TEACHER:

SONG:

BOOK:

MOVIE:

TV SHOW:

RADIO STATION:

CELEBRITY:

FEATURE:

THING TO DO ON THE WEEKEND:

STORE IN THE MALL:

OUTDOOR ACTIVITY:

FAMILY MEMBER:

ROOM IN MY HOUSE:

CHILDHOOD TOY:

TIME OF DAY:

FAMILY VACATION:

ARTICLE OF CLOTHING:

ACCESSORY:

NAME:

SUBJECT:

COLOR:

FOOD:

HOLIDAY:

ANIMAL:

SCHOOL LUNCH:

TEACHER:

SONG:

BOOK:

MOVIE:

TV SHOW:

RADIO STATION:

CELEBRITY:

FEATURE:

THING TO DO ON THE WEEKEND:

STORE IN THE MALL:

OUTDOOR ACTIVITY:

FAMILY MEMBER:

ROOM IN MY HOUSE:

CHILDHOOD TOY:

TIME OF DAY:

FAMILY VACATION:

ARTICLE OF CLOTHING:

ACCESSORY:

NAME:

SUBJECT: _____

COLOR: _____

FOOD: _____

HOLIDAY: _____

ANIMAL: _____

SCHOOL LUNCH: _____

TEACHER: _____

SONG: _____

BOOK: _____

MOVIE: _____

TV SHOW: _____

RADIO STATION: _____

CELEBRITY: _____

FEATURE: _____

THING TO DO ON THE WEEKEND: _____

STORE IN THE MALL: _____

OUTDOOR ACTIVITY: _____

FAMILY MEMBER: _____

ROOM IN MY HOUSE: _____

CHILDHOOD TOY: _____

TIME OF DAY: _____

FAMILY VACATION: _____

ARTICLE OF CLOTHING: _____

ACCESSORY: _____

More About Me:
Pure Niceness and Sensitivity

NAME:_____

My best feature is: _____

My grossest feature is:_____

What makes me:

Laugh so hard I snork through my nose? _____

Cry?_____ Smile? _____

Crazy?_____ Mad? _____

Embarrassed? _____

My favorite word is:_____

My favorite sound is:_____

Three things in my room that I wish weren't: _____

_____

My worst nightmare is: _____

_____

It would be totally cool if this dream came true: _____

_____

_____

I love my pet because: _____

I hate my pet because: _____

Which celebrity would star as me in the movie of my life?

_____

If I were an animal, I would be:_____

My sickest food ever is: _____

_____is cool. _____is cooler.

_____is dorky. _____is dorkier.

_____is unpleasant._____is unpleasanter.

16

nAmE:_____

My best feature is: _____

My grossest feature is: _____

What makes me:

Laugh so hard I snork through my nose? _____

Cry?_____ Smile? _____

Crazy?_____ Mad? _____

Embarrassed? _____

My favorite word is:_____

My favorite sound is:_____

Three things in my room that I wish weren't:_____

_____

My worst nightmare is: _____

_____

It would be totally cool if this dream came true:_____

_____

I love my pet because: _____

I hate my pet because: _____

Which celebrity would star as me in the movie of my life?

_____

If I were an animal, I would be: _____

My sickest food ever is: _____

_____is cool.   _____is cooler.

_____is dorky.   _____is dorkier.

_____is unpleasant. _____is unpleasanter.

NAME: _____

My best feature is: _____

My grossest feature is: _____

What makes me:

    Laugh so hard I snork through my nose? _____

    Cry? _____ Smile? _____

    Crazy? _____ Mad? _____

    Embarrassed? _____

My favorite word is: _____

My favorite sound is: _____

Three things in my room that I wish weren't: _____

_____

My worst nightmare is: _____

_____

It would be totally cool if this dream came true: _____

_____

I love my pet because: _____

I hate my pet because: _____

Which celebrity would star as me in the movie of my life?

_____

If I were an animal, I would be: _____

My sickest food ever is: _____

_____ is cool.   _____ is cooler.

_____ is dorky.   _____ is dorkier.

_____ is unpleasant. _____ is unpleasanter.

18

nAmE:_____

My best feature is: _____

My grossest feature is: _____

What makes me:

    Laugh so hard I snork through my nose?_____

    Cry?_____ Smile?_____

    Crazy?_____ Mad?_____

    Embarrassed?_____

My favorite word is:_____

My favorite sound is:_____

Three things in my room that I wish weren't:_____

_____

My worst nightmare is:_____

_____

It would be totally cool if this dream came true:_____

_____

_____

I love my pet because:_____

I hate my pet because:_____

Which celebrity would star as me in the movie of my life?

_____

If I were an animal, I would be:_____

My sickest food ever is:_____

_____ is cool.   _____ is cooler.

_____ is dorky.   _____ is dorkier.

_____ is unpleasant._____ is unpleasanter.

19

Would You Rather . . .

. . . kiss a frog or your Social Studies teacher?

NAME	ANSWER
:	
:	
:	

. . . be trapped all night in the cafeteria while the cafeteria monitor goes into detail about her intestinal problems, or be trapped in your room with your beagle after it has committed an **Odor Crime**?

NAME	ANSWER
:	
:	
:	

. . . watch someone who is so perfect that the word "perfect" is not perfect enough for her as she flirts with your crush, or get sent to the nurse's office for a little lie-down time on the cot during art class?

NAME	ANSWER
:	
:	
:	

TOTAL DUMBNESS

. . . chew on an already chewed-on pencil or run your fingernails down the chalkboard?

NAME		ANSWER
_____	:	_____
_____	:	_____
_____	:	_____
_____	:	_____

. . . get a makeover from the prettiest girl in the school, or give the prettiest girl in school a makeover?

NAME		ANSWER
_____	:	_____
_____	:	_____
_____	:	_____
_____	:	_____

. . . help your mom clean out the house for a garage sale, or watch your best friend freak out over a disruption in the precarious **Lunch Table Dynamic**?

NAME		ANSWER
_____	:	_____
_____	:	_____
_____	:	_____
_____	:	_____

OUR TURDY POSSESSIONS

. . . have your aunt work in the principal's office, or have old lady bloomers strewn across your lawn as a parade of classmates walks by?

NAME   ANSWER

_____ : _____
_____ : _____
_____ : _____

CAUGHT TONGING THE DAINTIES

. . . be related to your worst enemy, or never be able to wash your hair again?

NAME   ANSWER

_____ : _____
_____ : _____
_____ : _____

. . . experience pure love for someone with the nickname "Butt Buttlington," or be the object of pure love from T.U.K.W.N.I.F., That Ugly Kid Whose Name I Forget?

NAME   ANSWER

_____ : _____
_____ : _____
_____ : _____

TUKWNIF

... eat your school's meat loaf, or have a live earthworm taped inside your mouth?

NAME		ANSWER
	:
	:
	:
	:

... get a massage from Dracula, or have a group of teachers in your house?

NAME		ANSWER
	:
	:
	:
	:

... have a totally cute adorable kitten as a pet or a koala?

NAME		ANSWER
	:
	:
	:
	:

Everybody Now!

With all of your friends, name five things that are even creepier than clowns:

_____

_____

_____

_____

_____

Name at least two things you can't remember if you heard or made up:

_____

_____

_____

_____

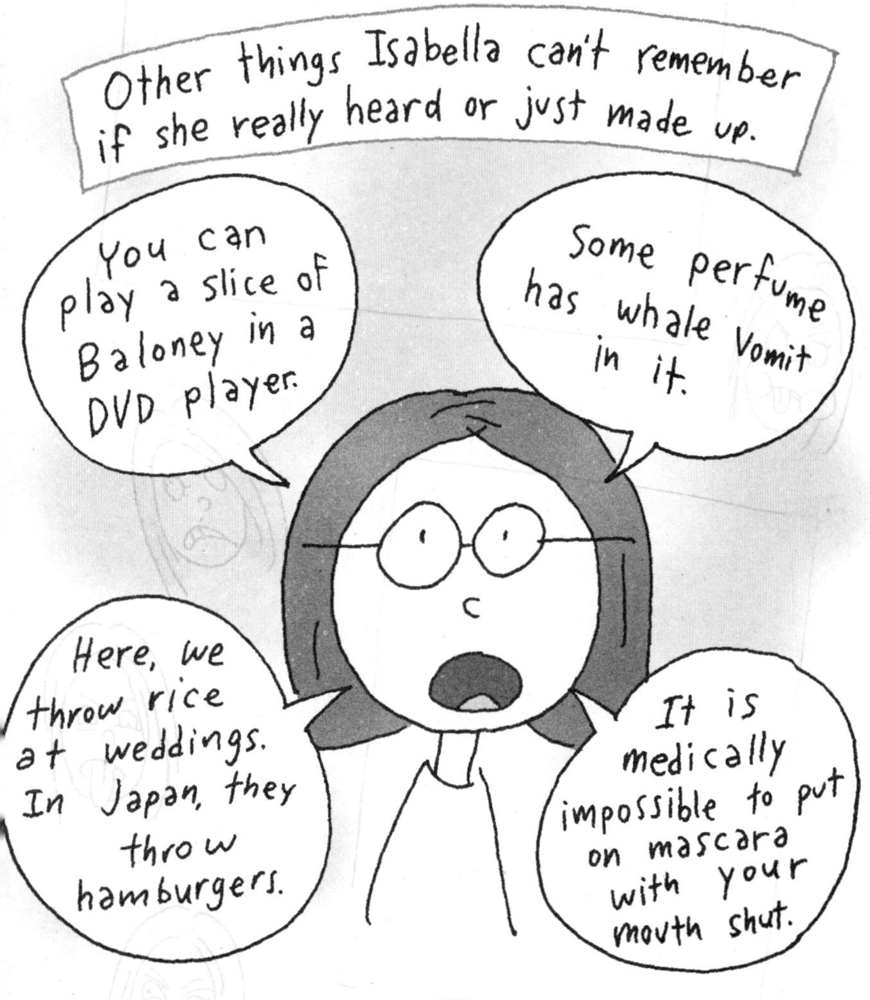
Other things Isabella can't remember if she really heard or just made up.
You can play a slice of Baloney in a DVD player.
Some perfume has whale vomit in it.
Here, we throw rice at weddings. In Japan, they throw hamburgers.
It is medically impossible to put on mascara with your mouth shut.

Draw your dirtiest looks here:

I'm angry on the outside, but I'm far angrier on the inside.

27

Otherwordly Garment Spookiness

HAUNTED PANTS
(I CAN PROVE THESE)

POSSESSED UNDERWEAR
(THESE SEEM LIKELY)

VOODOO
MUUMUU,
(I HOPE THESE
EXIST. IT'S A
GOOD RHYME)

Do you believe in ghosts? Why or why not?

List three times when screaming is totally necessary:

_____

_____

_____

Other times when screaming is necessary....

Monster is chasing you and your high heels are too cute to abandon

Eaten by Ants

Gramps accidentally shoots a moon

The Mom Factor

"Mom says that nobody, anywhere, can ever make you crazy like a relative. Not a friend, not an enemy, **NOBODY**."

Jamie Kelly

What does your mom do that's totally embarrassing?

_____

_____

_____

_____

What's the best thing about your mom?

_____

_____

_____

_____

OKAY. MOMS ARE GOOD FOR CERTAIN THINGS. LIKE...

They give you cash!

they seem to enjoy cleaning

The Dad Factor

Does your dad do any of these humiliating things in front of your friends? Or something **WORSE**?

DANCES

permits self to be witnessed in bathing suit.

Dresses like Lady for Halloween

Talks

What's your favorite thing about your dad?

Where do your friends rank?

Spill it! It's time to rate your friends. Who is most likely to . . .

. . . eat the meat loaf at school? _____

. . . set a fashion trend? _____

. . . write a love poem? _____

. . . participate in a Walk-A-Thon? _____

. . . color her contact lenses with a marker? _____

. . . bust out a righteous dance move? _____

. . . create a sculpture out of her lunch? _____

SQUEAK SQUEAK

ONLY ISABELLA AND
SPACE ALIENS ARE CAPABLE
OF DOING THIS

. . . try a new flavor of Lip Smacker? _____

. . . try dyeing her hair? _____

. . . say something nice to the Mean Office Lady? _____

. . . shave her stuffed animals? _____

. . . sneak a peek in someone else's diary? _____

. . . steal the permanent record of her worst enemy?

_____

. . . put her irresistability powers into action? _____

. . . lick a hairbrush to see what it tastes like? _____

. . . convince her dog to run away? _____

Circle the answers that apply! Are you and your friends good-looking enough to:

A) Put mayonnaise on your popcorn?

B) Step right on a fish?

C) Eat salad for breakfast?

D) All of the above

E) None of the above

Are you and your friends NOT attractive enough to:

A) Burn down SeaWorld?

B) Brush your teeth with ketchup?

C) Be a waitress?

D) All of the above

E) None of the above

"Here's a drawing of me having it going on. (I think I may also be all up in that, but I'm not sure exactly what that means.)"

Jamie Kelly

PROBABLY JEALOUS

Pure Ugliness you have seen:

Beauty is only skin deep, but hate goes all the way to the bone.

Pure Beauty you have seen:

GORGEOUS
PRETTY
SLIGHTLY CUTE
PLAIN
UGLY
WOOF

BEAUTY

BEAUTY

Which phrases best describe you and your friends?
(Check off any that apply.)

- ☐ Clean, lovely, and bright
- ☐ Pretty enough to be a shoe salesperson
- ☐ The Smartest Chicks in the World
- ☐ Mega-popular
- ☐ Pure love and joy
- ☐ Pretty enough to be a figure skater
- ☐ Full of inner beauty
- ☐ Full of outer beauty
- ☐ When I stand next to something, I make it look less pretty by comparison
- ☐ More glamorous than a movie star holding two puppies

Which phrases best describe the kids in your class?
(Check off any that apply.)

- ◯ Second filthiest
- ◯ Not the dumbest
- ◯ Conceited
- ◯ Utterly disgusting
- ◯ Okay, I guess
- ◯ Stuck-up
- ◯ Mostly gross
- ◯ The pit of unpopularity
- ◯ Could be worse

Isabella's Popularity-o-Meter

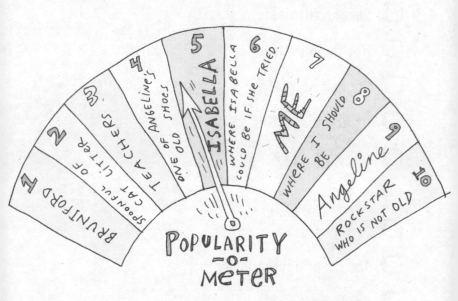

1. BRUNIFORD
2. SPOONFUL OF CAT LITTER
3. TEACHERS
4. ONE OF ANGELINE'S OLD SHOES
5. ISABELLA
ISABELLA: WHERE ISABELLA COULD BE IF SHE TRIED.
6. ME
7. WHERE I SHOULD BE
8.
9. Angeline
10. ROCKSTAR WHO IS NOT OLD

POPULARITY -o- METER

Perfect people make me perfectly ill.

Where Do You Fall?

Use the Popularity-o-Meter to rank yourself! Then rank
your friends, and see how the numbers match up.

NAME	SELF-RANKING	FRIEND	FRIEND	FRIEND

Add one bonus point if you're filling this out while
dancing. Lose one point if it's square dancing.

With your **BFF**s fill in the five most popular people in your school:

5. _____

4. _____

3. _____

2. _____

1. _____

Now fill in the five most popular lunch meats in your school:

5. _____

4. _____

3. _____

2. _____

1. _____

"Isabella used this opportunity to share with me (**again**) more about her theories on Popularity. She says that Unpopularity is contagious, and you can catch it the same way you catch the **Flu** or **Bad Dancing**. Honestly, though, I don't believe that Unpopularity is a real Force of Nature, like Gravity or Deliciousness.

   Isabella will probably be a Professor of Popularity Science one day."

Jamie Kelly

ISABELLA'S LOSER SCALE

FROM BAD TO WORSE

DINK — PESTY, PARTIALLY STINKY

DORK — LOUD, OFTEN OAFISH.

DORKBAG — SPITTY-MOUTHED. LIKES TO LIE. TWITCHY.

TURD — MEAN AND THICK-HEADED. QUESTIONABLE SHOE CHOICES.

BLONDWAD — STEALER OF BALM FLAVORS. POSSIBLY UNFAMILIAR WITH SOAP.

TURDPIE — BIG-TIME ANNOYING. FUTURE CANNIBAL. UNFLATTERING WARDROBE.

Do you know anyone who ranks on this highly scientific scale?

Name: _____
Ranking: _____

Name: _____
Ranking: _____

Name: _____
Ranking: _____

Name: _____
Ranking: _____

Name: _____
Ranking: _____

Name: _____
Ranking: _____

Name: _____
Ranking: _____

People you and your friends don't care about at all:

For example:

George Washington, Ringo Starr,
Christina Aguilera, Zeus, Angeline,
Dan Rather, Caesar Riley,
Angeline, Paul Bunyan, Cleopatra,
Nefertiti, Maria Barbo, Angeline,
koko the signing Gorilla, The
Yellow Teletubby, Angeline,
Angeline, Angeline, Angeline
ANGELINE

Crimes Against Popularity that have occurred in your school:

Example: Nicknaming

_____

_____

_____

_____

_____

One second Before
You get a Nickname

One Second After
You get a Nickname

Nicknaming

Almost the Worst Thing That Can Happen to You in Middle School

Have you ever had a nickname? What is it? What is the worst nickname anyone in your school has?

School prepares you for the real world, which also bites.

49

Boys

A.K.A. Potential Victims of Pure Beauty

THE SCIENCE OF BOY-OLOGY
Local Specimens

CHIP
CUTENESS RANKING: **1**

NON-MEAN AND HANDSOME ENOUGH TO BE IN A SHAVING CREAM COMMERCIAL

HUDSON RIVERS
CUTENESS RANKING: **8**
EASILY TRICKED INTO Thinking ANGELINE IS PRETTY. OTHERWISE EXCELLENT

ROSCO
(CHIP'S DOG)
CUTENESS RANKING: **19**

STRICTLY SPEAKING NOT A BOY, BUT CUTER AND WAY MORE POPULAR THAN MOST TRUE BOYS

MIKE PINSETTI
CUTENESS RANKING: **ALMOST LAST**

MEAN AND MOUTHY. IF YOU MEET HIM TELL HIM ALL ABOUT SOAP.

THAT ONE KID
CUTENESS RANKING: **LAST**

DOES HE EVEN HAVE A NAME? WHO KNOWS. HE DOESN'T SEEM TO NEED ONE

Where do the boys in your school fall on this highly scientific chart?

CUTENESS RANKING:
1

CUTENESS RANKING: **8**

CUTENESS RANKING: **19**

CUTENESS RANKING:
ALMOST LAST

CUTENESS RANKING: LAST

Name your dream date!

NAME	ANSWER
:	
:	
:	
:	

"I wonder how old you are when people start checking
you out. I wonder how old you are when they stop
checking you out. More than that, I wonder exactly how
you perform a checking out, and how you receive one.
I'm going to make Stinker check me out and try to see
how I look in the mirror while he does it. **Shut Up.**
It's not weird to force your beagle to check you out.
Probably lots of people do it."

Jamie Kelly

What boys definitely have crushes on you?

NAME	ANSWER
:	
:	
:	
:	

What makes you so irresistible?

NAME	ANSWER
:	
:	
:	
:	

If your crush wrote you a note, what would it say?

Love is in the air,
so you might just want
to stay inside.

Middle School Mania

Name five things that are in your locker that shouldn't be:

Do teachers fart?

_____

_____

_____

_____

"TEACHERS DON'T FART.

I spend something like **eight months** a year,
seven hours a day with teachers. If they did,
I'd know it. Moms do it. Dads do it. Beagles do it
(sometimes so bad that your eyes burn and your lungs
might try to escape by jumping out your mouth)."

Jamie Kelly

Who is your **BTF**? (like a **BFF**, but for teachers)

_____

_____

_____

_____

The Unpleasantness

"Now, before I tell you about **The Unpleasantness**, Dumb Diary, you should know that I was not trying to get in trouble. It just sort of happened.

Here is a transcript of the exchange:

ISABELLA: So, what sort of animals are we learning about today, Mr. VanDoy?

VANDOY: I'm not quite sure. I've been very busy at home and I got a little behind.

ME: It doesn't look so little to me.

It happened so fast that I hardly knew I had said it. Isabella's huge whooping laugh and calls of "**Oh no, you dinnit**" did not help things, and Mr. VanDoy sent me with a note, to the office." *Jamie Kelly*

well c'mon.
it doesn't.

FESS UP: What was YOUR most embarrassing teacher moment?

What's the craziest thing that ever happened on a school field trip?

I'm happy. Don't wreck it by talking.

What's the **WORST** thing you ever had to go to the nurse's office for?

_____

_____

_____

_____

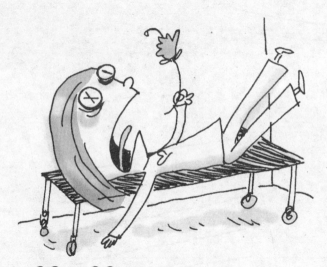

GROSSNESS ALERT: Have you ever thrown up in school?

_____

_____

_____

WARNING! Beware of **GIGGLECIDE**: That thing where somebody grabs you by the shoulders and makes little stampy stomps and shakes their head around and squeals those happy, giggly, shrill sounds that make puppies pee. You sort of feel like you've been playfully mauled by a really adorable grizzly.

Times you've been the victim of Gigglecide:

_____

_____

_____

_____

Gym

An Excuse to Make Kids Sweat in the Middle of the School Day

"The teamwork exercise in gym class today was this: The little groups race one another in an exercise called **Sled Dogs**. One person sits on the floor on a towel and grabs on to a broom while the other members of the team drag him or her across the gym. Each person takes a turn on the towel. I guess this is to determine who is good at thinking up an excuse to not have to participate in gym that day."

Jamie Kelly

WHEEZE   HUFF PUFF   GRUNT

REAL SLED DOGS BEING TOTALLY EMBARRASSED FOR US

What's the worst thing you ever had to do for gym class?

It's a jungle out there, and it doesn't smell so great in here either.

Eat at Your Own Risk

List the top three grossest things your school cafeteria serves, if you can narrow it down:

3. _____

2. _____

1. _____

Draw your cafeteria monitor here!

"You remember Bruntford, don't you Dumb Diary? She is the water buffalo that somebody trained to be a cafeteria monitor and whose job it is to make sure that everything in the lunchroom flows as smoothly as gravy through a grandma. **Ugh!** I think I just grossed myself out a little. I'm sure off gravy for a while."

Jamie Kelly

Note supernatural resemblance of Bruntford to Meat loaf

Lunch Table Dynamics

"Angeline was at our table today. I had no idea why she decided to sit with Isabella and me, but Angeline can sit anywhere she wants. She is immune, it seems, to **The Rules of the Lunchroom Tables**. (There's a cool kid table, a jerk table, a computer kid table . . . . you get the picture.)"

Jamie Kelly

Angeline and Meat LoAf

UcK.

If you could give your lunch table a name, what would it be?

_____

_____

_____

_____

Your lunch table dynamic is, like, one of the most important parts of your day. Who sits at your table?

_____

_____

_____

_____

_____

_____

Who definitely does **NOT** sit at your table, ever?

_____

_____

_____

What are the **Top Ten** worst things about your school?
Fill them in with your friends!

10. _____

9. _____

8. _____

7. _____

6. _____

5. _____

4. _____

3. _____

2. _____

1. _____

Here are some of the worst things about Mackerel Middle School:

When the Bus Drivers dress up for Halloween

When the teachers try talking cool

The unmistakable tangy flavor of horse organs in the cafeteria meatloaf.

If YOU Ruled the School . . .

If you were in charge, what things would you and your friends add to your school? Soda machines? Roller coasters on the playground? Makeover classes? List 'em here.

_____

_____

_____

_____

_____

_____

_____

_____

_____

Other Things OUR SCHOOL SHOULD BUY

Adorable
Uniforms
for the
female
custodians

A
Puppy to
live inside
every
locker

ZAP

DRINKING FOUNTAINS
THAT LASER-BEAM
PEOPLE THAT SPIT
THEIR GUM OUT
IN THEM

Saturdays Rule!

"Saturdays are so cool that I will never ever figure out why they only made one of them per week. Here's my idea for a whole new lineup of days:"

SATURDAY
I can't improve on Saturday so I'm not changing it.

SUNTURDAY
This will be another Saturday, but it will also have the aimless Quality of a Sunday.

MONTURDAY
You can't get all your fun into just two Saturdays, so this is a bonus third.

WEEKSDAY
NOBODY LIKES WEEKDAYS. (THAT'S WHY THEY'RE CALLED "WEAK DAYS") LET'S GET THEM ALL OVER IN A SINGLE DAY.

FRIDAY
OK, IT'S A WEEKDAY BUT FRIDAYS ARE VERY IMPORTANT FOR PLANNING YOUR SATURDAYS.

FRIDAYNIGHTDAY
THIS IS AN ENTIRE DAY THAT'S NOTHING BUT FRIDAY NIGHT, ALL DAY LONG.

Jamie Kelly

What are your favorite things to do with your friends on the weekends (or on any of these new days of the week)? Fill in the chart together!

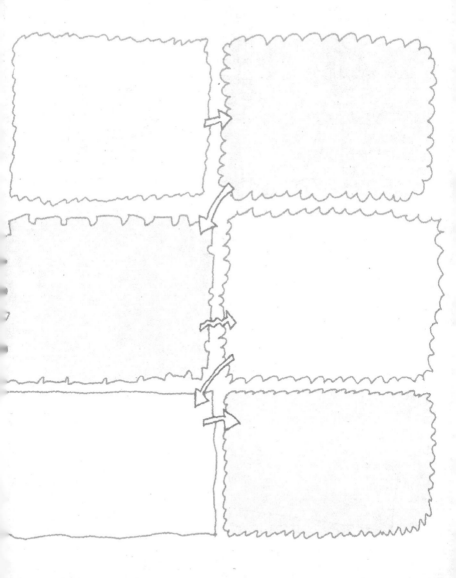

If the days of the week were people, who would they be?

if days were people....

Saturday   Sunday   Wednesday

MONDAY

TUESDAY

WEDNESDAY

THURSDAY

FRIDAY

SATURDAY

SUNDAY

WARNING: Grossness Ahead!

ways I have grossed myself out.

Looked up nose with MIRROR AND FLASHLIGHT. (GROSSED OUT FOR 3 HOURS.)

CONVINCED MYSELF THAT SPAGHETTI LOOKED LiKE VEiNS.

(GROSSED OUT ON SPAGHETTI FOR 4 MONTHS)

FORGOT TO LOOK AWAY WHEN PARENTS KiSSED. (STiLL GROSSED OUT BUT IT ALSO MAKES ME LAUGH A LiTTLE)

What are some ways that you've grossed yourself out?

Beautification!

Combine any two of the words below to describe your hair color:

Glorious Heavenly Sunshine
Groundhog
Flawless
Moldy
Goldenrod
Perfection
Caramel
Dull
Perfect blond
Chocolate
Raven
Shiny
Raw chicken
Glistening
Clumpy
Fire-engine
Dry
Spectacular
Not quite brown

NAME   HAIR COLOR

_____   _____

_____   _____

_____   _____

_____   _____

Your Signature Flavor

"Isabella's lips cleared up a couple hours after lunch. It was like a miracle. They turned from what looked like sad little splintered slivers of beef jerky into what looks like full, ripe luscious crescents of papaya.

It was the meat loaf. The mysterious meat it's made from had some sort of incredible healing power on Isabella's lips. And it's her new signature flavor. She stuffed a wad of it into an old lip-balm tube. I know. It's awful. But it smells better than ChocoMint."

Jamie Kelly

If you could invent your own signature lip balm flavor, what would it be?

NAME   FLAVOR

_____   _____

_____   _____

_____   _____

NOW GET CREATIVE!

What are some other uses for lip balm?

_____

_____

_____

_____

If you're stranded without lip balm or your other favorite cosmetics, how can you improvise? Good & Plenty® or lollipops can turn your lips cool colors. And it never hurts to have some extra magic barrettes in your backpack, just in case. List your genius ideas here!

_____

_____

_____

_____

Known Experts on Fashion

A fashion blunder can make or break your rank on the Popularity-o-Meter, so it's important to know what to wear and where to wear it!

PHASES IN THE LIFE of PANTS

PHASE 1
Brand new and in style. Happiest time in a pant's life. Wear at any time.

PHASE 2
Slightly out of style or with taco stain. Wear on Sundays only.

PHASE 3
Hole bitten out of fanny by dog or tailor. Wear only as part of Hobo costume.

What's your favorite Friday outfit?

_____

_____

What's your favorite "Never Leave the House in This" outfit?

_____

_____

Accessorizing is an important part of any outfit. The possibilities are endless!

More Glamorous Jewelry From Old Games

Spooky Voodoo Necklace made from old Operation™ Game Bones

Pierced earrings made from Mr. Potato Head's™ Ears

What other kinds of jewelry could you make from things lying around your house?

_____

_____

_____

_____

Design your ideal outfit below. Then, on the next page, draw what's **REALLY** in your closet!

I'm not spoiled. I deserve all my stuff.

85

Makeovers

They totally work!

My Incredible Makeup Skills at Work

 Frankenstein

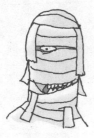 The Mummy

 Wolfman

Jamie and Isabella, Makeover Masters: Project Margaret

"Then I heard something that I had never heard before. It's not a sound you often hear. It was sort of a soft, wet, popping sound. I realize now that it was the sound of twenty-six jaws dropping open at exactly the same time.

Margaret was, well, she was **GORGEOUS**. Her hair, her perfume, her jewelry, her new clothes, were working together like a symphony orchestra comprised of the rare supermodels who are smart enough to read music."

Jamie Kelly

AN EXCELLENT MOM MAKEOVER

If you could give anyone a makeover, who would it be?

_____

_____

_____

Draw yourself in one of the boxes below. Then let your friends draw on your picture to give you a complete makeover! Rate the makeover on a scale of 1 to 10.

BeFoRe MAKEoveR

WORN UP IN PROM STYLE

BRAiDS

GLAMoRoUS WAVE

Don't try this at home!

RANKiNG

RANKING

RANKING

RANKING

And now for something REALLY fun . . .

Give Angeline a makeUNDER. Don't hold back!

Starter
Angeline:

Some ideas:

COLOR OF EYES MEDICALLY CHANGED FROM BABY BLUE TO BABY BARF

GLORIOUS MANE OF SILKEN GOLD REPLACED WITH COARSE TUFT OF BRISTLES FROM WARTHOG BUTT.

NO LONGER ALLOWED TO GO BY LOVELY NAME OF "ANGELINE." NOW HER OFFICIAL LEGAL NAME IS SOMETHING LIKE "CANKER SORE" OR "SMEAR!"

The only good thing about Angeline is that she can never bother me more than she does right now.

Inner Beauty

So we all know you're beautiful on the outside. But what about your inner beauty? Test it here! You can each pick one of the four shapes as your check box, and check off any questions you would answer YES to.

Have you ever cheated on a test or homework?

Would you ever tell on a friend?

Would you re-tell?

Do you have a best enemy?

Have you ever broken a Mean Office Lady's hip?

Have you ever been sent to the principal's office?

Have you ever gotten detention?

Scoring:

6-7 checks: Inner beauty? What's that?

3-5 checks: You have a healthy amount of inner beauty. Not as much as Angeline, but you can't win 'em all.

0-2 checks: Your inner beauty is so inflamed that it has ruptured through your skin and spewed bubbling squirts of beauty all over you!

BONUS: What's the worst lie you've ever told?

NAME	ANSWER
:	
:	
:	
:	

BFFs

All **BFF**s have their own secret language that only they understand. What are some of your favorite words, terms, and inside jokes?

_____

_____

_____

_____

_____

_____

_____

_____

_____

Confession Session!

What is the biggest trouble you and your friends ever got in? What for?

_____

_____

_____

_____

List your best schemes here:

_____

_____

_____

Some of Isabella's Schemes

Tried to fly
with Balloons.
(first grade)

Attempted to achieve
tan with flashlights.
(wasted over 40 batteries)

Masqueraded as
weathergirl to
try to get principal
to declare snow day
in May.

Spying

Different from Stalking

"Pretending to be asleep is just about the best way to eavesdrop as long as you do it well. Don't scrunch your eyes closed too hard, and don't snore like they do in cartoons."

Jamie Kelly

Who have you committed spying against? Was it successful?

_____

_____

_____

_____

_____

Don't forget, disguises are usually a pretty good idea when spying. What would your ultimate disguise be? Draw it!

Total Experts

"I can make a valentine that would make an ant fall in love with an aardvark. What are you really great at?"

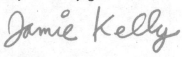

YOU ARE SO LOVELY THAT I WILL NOT SNORK YOU UP MY NOSE

NAME : ANSWER

_____ : _____

_____ : _____

_____ : _____

_____ : _____

Which of the following best describes you?

GLITTER ARTIST
or
ARTISTICALLY IMPAIRED

Prove it! Break out your private glitter blends and demonstrate your best Glitterification skills below.

Can you create something spectacular out of something that other people would overlook? Write or draw it here!

Alternate uses for a regular old napkin:

"The Tent"
Good for hiding a more massive icky OBJECT.

"The BANDITO"
useful to conceal your identity as you sneak away from the table.

Endless skills

"I know what you're thinking, Dumb Diary. You're thinking, **'Wow, Jamie, you're totally pretty and a really good dancer.'** I'm not going to tell you you're wrong, Dumb Diary, but please, try to stay on the subject."

Jamie Kelly

Draw a picture of you and your friends dancing!

"My social studies teacher, Mr. VanDoy, never smiles. I know that's hard to believe, because everybody smiles about something, right? I wonder if when you become an adult, you can lose your sense of humor the way you lose your teeth or hair or fashion sense."

Jamie Kelly

What are some of the craziest things you and your friends have seen adults do?

_____

_____

_____

_____

Name some ways adults are like animals:

_____

_____

_____

_____

_____

_____

_____

They are LARGE AND GROSSLY HAIRY.

when they sing along to their favorite songs, many sound like a Hog Being Dragged by its tail.

Adultness

It Could Eventually Happen to You

When you're not being a supermodel/scientist who acts on the side, what do you want to do when you grow up?

NAME	ANSWER

Would you rather . . .

. . . be a professional dancer/singer, or star in your own hit TV show?

NAME	ANSWER

. . . create beautiful works of art, or design shoes for celebrities?

NAME	ANSWER

Notes to Our Future Selves

Three things we will never do to our kids:

1. _____

2. _____

3. _____

Three things we will never wear:

1. _____

2. _____

3. _____

Three things we will never make our kids wear:

1. _____

2. _____

3. _____

What goes around, comes around and when it does, duck.

Three things we will never make our kids eat:

1.

2.

3.

Three things we will never make our kids do:

1.

2.

3.

Three fun things we did with our friends that we will never forget:

1.

2.

3.

Three things we will never stop doing:

1.

2.

3.

Can't get enough of Jamie Kelly?
Check out her other Dear Dumb Diary books!

#1 LET'S PRETEND
THIS NEVER HAPPENED

#2 MY PANTS
ARE HAUNTED!

#3 AM I THE PRINCESS
OR THE FROG?

#4 NEVER DO
ANYTHING, EVER

#5 CAN ADULTS
BECOME HUMAN?

#6 THE PROBLEM
WITH HERE IS THAT IT'S
WHERE I'M FROM

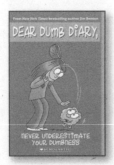

#7 NEVER
UNDERESTIMATE
YOUR DUMBNESS

#8 IT'S NOT MY FAULT
I KNOW EVERYTHING

OUR DUMB DIARY:
A JOURNAL TO SHARE

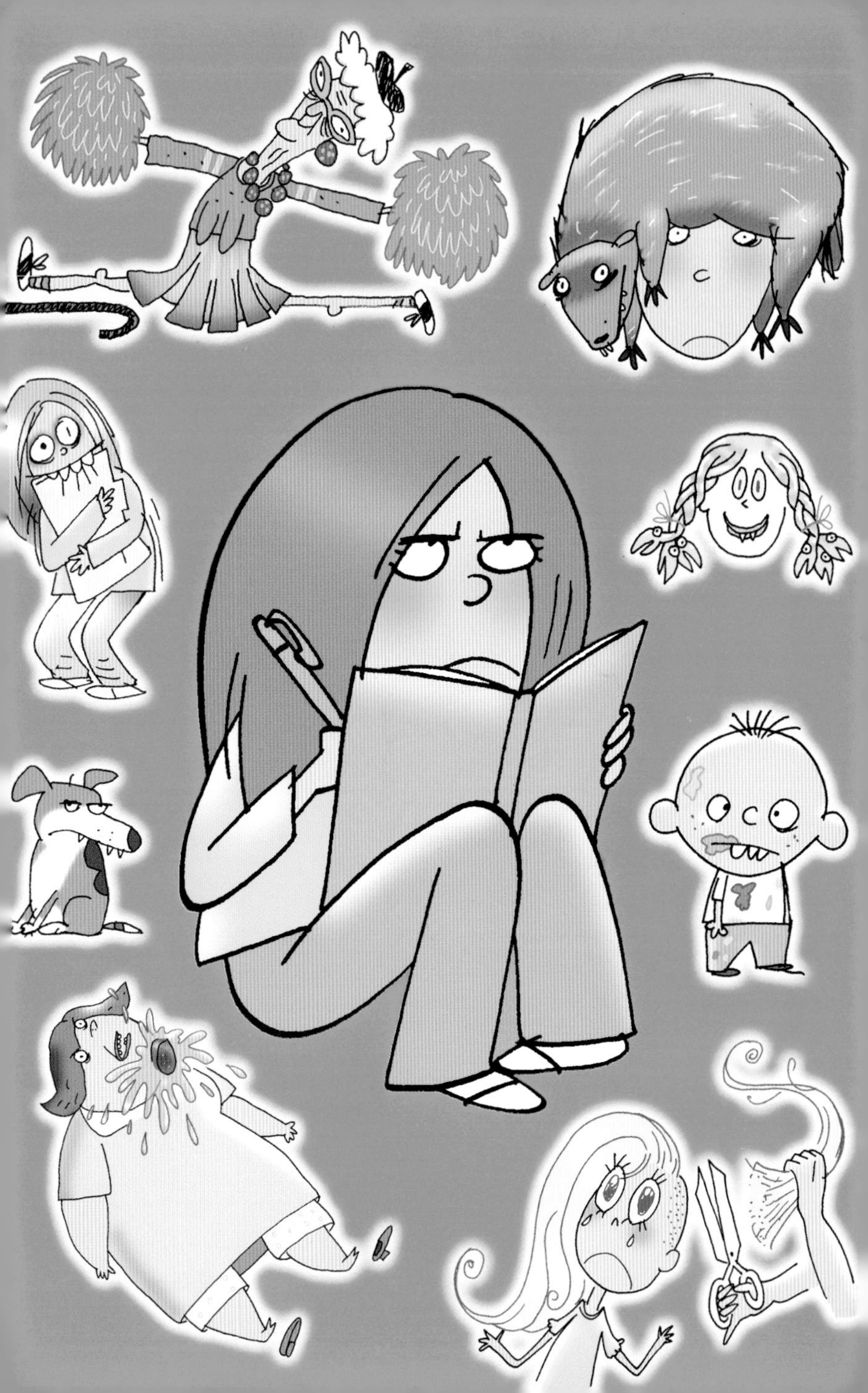

LET'S PRETEND
THIS NEVER HAPPENED

Think you can handle another Jamie Kelly diary?

Jim Benton's Tales from Mackerel Middle School

DEAR DUMB DIARY,

LET'S PRETEND THIS NEVER HAPPENED

BY JAMIE KELLY

SCHOLASTIC INC.

New York   Toronto   London   Auckland   Sydney
Mexico City   New Delhi   Hong Kong   Buenos Aires

ISBN 0-439-62904-7

Copyright © 2004 by Jim Benton
All rights reserved. Published by Scholastic Inc.
SCHOLASTIC, APPLE, and associated logos are trademarks
and/or registered trademarks of Scholastic, Inc.

12 11 10 9 8 7 6 5 4 3   4 5 6 7 8 9/0
Printed in China   40
First Scholastic Printing, July 2004

For
everybody that is in,
or will be in,
or has ever been in,
middle school.

Special thanks to: Craig Walker, Steve Scott, Susan Jeffers Casel, Shannon Penney.

And especially to editor Maria Barbo who really and truly knows her way around middle school.

This DiARY PROPERTY OF

Jamie Kelly

SCHOOL: MACKEREL MIDDLE SCHOOL

LOCKER: 101

BEST FRIEND: Isabella

PET: STinker which is a beagle

EYE COLOR: Green

HAIR COLOR: ~~Brown~~ Brownishly Blond with Brunette Brownness

WARNING

READ NO FURTHER

The
Last
Person
Who
Kept
Reading →

THiS iS NOT
YOUR DIARY

I CAN TELL

Dear Whoever Is Reading My Dumb Diary,

Are you sure you're supposed to be reading somebody else's diary? Maybe I told you that you could, so that's okay. But if you are Angeline, I did NOT give you permission, so stop it.

If you are my parents, then YES, I know that I am not allowed to call people idiots and fools and goons and halfwits and pinheads and all that, but this is a diary, and I didn't actually "call" them anything. I *wrote* it. And if you punish me for it, then I will know that you read my diary, which I am *not* giving you permission to do.

Now, by the power vested in me, I do promise that everything in this diary is true or, at least, as true as I think it needs to be.

Signed,

Jamie Kelly

PS: If this is you, Angeline, reading this, then HA-HA! I got you! For I have written this in poison ink on a special poison paper, and you had better run and call 911 right now!

PSS: If this is you, Hudson, reading this, I have an antidote to the poison and it is conveniently available to you through a simple phone call to my house. But don't mention the poison thing to my parents if they answer. I think they might be all weird about me poisoning people.

Here they ARE
DISAPPROVING poISONING

Monday 02

Dear Dumb Diary,

I was out playing with my beagle, Stinker, this afternoon and I was doing that thing where you pretend to throw the ball and then don't throw it and Stinker starts running for it until he realizes you didn't really throw it at all. Usually I only do it two or three times but today I guess I was thinking about something else, because when I finally realized that I hadn't thrown the ball yet, I had probably done it about a hundred and forty times. Stinker was a little bit cross-eyed and foamy and he wouldn't come back in the house for a long time.

I wonder if dogs can hold a grudge.

Frustration Foam

Tuesday 03

Dear Dumb Diary,

    I think I was very nearly *nicknamed* today, which is almost the worst thing that can happen to you in middle school. I was eating a peach at lunch and another peach fell out of my bag onto the floor, and Mike Pinsetti, who only breathes through his mouth, was standing there and he said, "Hey, Peach Girl."

    He's pretty much the official nicknamer of the school, and Pinsetti's labels, although stupid, often stick. (Don't believe me, Diary? Just ask old "Butt Buttlington," who was one of Pinsetti's very first nicknames. I don't even know his real name. Nobody does. He's been called Butt Buttlington for so long that his mom actually called him Butt by accident one time when she dropped him off at school. "Bye, Butt Buttlington," she said. Then when she realized what she had done, she tried to make it better by following up with: "We're proud of you.")

One second before
you get a nickname

One second after
you get a nickname

Back to my peach story. I picked the backstabbing fruit up real quick. I thought nobody had heard Pinsetti, which pretty much cancels out a nickname. But then this adorable musical laughter that sounds like somebody is tickling a baby by rubbing its tummy with a puppy comes from behind me. When I turn around, I see it's none other than Angeline, who was probably evilly committing this nickname to memory.

It's only a matter of time before I have to start signing my homework as PEACH GIRL.

Wednesday 04

Dear Dumb Diary,

Today Hudson Rivers (eighth cutest guy in my grade) talked to me in the hall. Normally, this would have no effect on me at all, since there is still a chance that Cute Guys One Through Seven might actually talk to me one day. But when Hudson said, "Hey," today, I could tell that he was totally in love with me, and I felt that I had an obligation to be irresistible for his benefit.

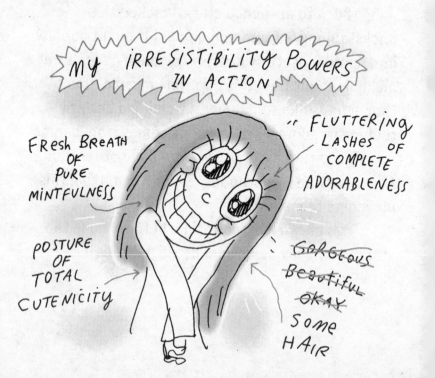

MY IRRESISTIBILITY POWERS IN ACTION

FRESH BREATH OF PURE MINTFULNESS

"FLUTTERING LASHES OF COMPLETE ADORABLENESS

POSTURE OF TOTAL CUTENICITY

~~GORGEOUS~~ ~~Beautiful~~ ~~OKAY~~ SOME HAIR

So just as I'm about to say something cool back to Hudson (Maybe even something REALLY cool. We'll never know for sure now.), Angeline comes around the corner with her jillion cute things dangling from her backpack, and intentionally looks cute RIGHT IN FRONT OF HIS EYES. This scorpion-like behavior on her part made me forget what I was going to say, so the only thing that came out of my mouth was a gush of air without any words in it. Not like this mattered, because he was staring at Angeline the same way Stinker was staring at the ball a couple days ago.

STINKER   HUDSON

It was pretty obvious that all of his love for me was squirting out his ears all over the floor. Ask Isabella if you don't believe me. She was standing right there.

As if that wasn't vicious enough, get this:

He says to Angeline: "Wow, is that your Lip Smacker I smell? ChocoMint? It's great."

Angeline stops for just a second and **LOOKS RIGHT AT ISABELLA AND ME.** Then she says to Hudson, "Yeah, it is." And her radiant smile freezes him in his tracks.

Frankly, I think that it is just rude and obscene to have teeth white enough to hurt and maybe **PERMANENTLY DAMAGE** the eyes of onlookers.

HAZARDOUS
DAZZLING
WHITENESS RAYS

AAAAAAAGH!!

SIZZLE

(In case my children are reading this years from now, this is the exact moment Angeline stole your father, Hudson, from me, and it is her fault that now your last name is Rumpelstiltskin or Schwarzenegger or Buttlington.)

SAD SAD FUTURE BABY LEARNING that his father has been STOLEN

DUMB DIARY

Angeline's fault

Here's the thing: Isabella is the **ONLY** girl in the entire school who uses ChocoMint Lip Smacker. It's the grossest flavor they ever made, but she **needed** her very own unique Lip Smacker flavor, and so she settled on the only one nobody else likes. All the girls know it's hers. Even Angeline knows it.

So Dumb Diary, let's see that scene again in slow motion: Suddenly, in one swift move, Angeline had stolen my future prom date/boyfriend/ husband, and Isabella had lost her signature Lip Smacker scent. (Isabella would rather wear her grandma's giant-bottomed pants to school than let anyone think she is copying Angeline.)

A MYSTERY of NATURE

ISABELLA'S HUMAN-SIZED BUTT

ISABELLA'S GRANDMA'S HORSE-LIKE BUTT

I suppose I could have said something, but I knew that Angeline had the "Peach Girl" nickname loaded in her Imaginary Slingshot of Pure Wickedness and was ready to let me have it right in front of Hudson.

I was powerless.

Of course, Dumb Diary, you understand that I'm **DESTROYED**. What you may not fully appreciate is the impact this scandalous event is having on Isabella. She is **EXTREMELY** smell-oriented, and not really well-equipped to change her scented ointments. I foresee a long, painful bout with chapped lips in her future.

It also occurs to me, Dumb Diary, that Angeline is so perfect that the word "perfect" is probably not perfect enough for her. One day they'll have to invent another word for her and when they do I hope it rhymes with vomit or turd because I think I have a good idea for a song if they do.

PRINCESS TURD OF TURDSYLVANIA

Wednesday, The Evening Edition

Dear Dumb Diary,

    Tonight at dinner, Mom announced that we're going to be taking care of my little cousin in a few weeks. He's, like, my aunt's daughter's brother's nephew or something.

    I know that your uncle's kids are your cousins, but then there are things like first cousins and second cousins and cousins once-removed. What does that mean? "Cousins once-removed."

    I had a wart once removed.

cousin
once-removed

wart
once removed

And, Dumb Diary, just to update you on Mom's Latest Food-Crime, last night she made a casserole with 147 ingredients, and it still tasted bad. It's hard to believe that out of 147 ingredients, not one of them tasted good.

Of course I ate it anyway. If you don't eat it, Mom gives you the speech on hard work and how the hungry children in Wheretheheckistan would just love her casserole.

It seems to me the kids in Wheretheheckistan have enough problems without dumping Mom's casseroles on them, too.

Thursday 05

Dear Dumb Diary,

   Because of Angeline, who thinks she is The Prettiest Girl in the World but probably is not even in the top five, I had to buy my lunch at school today. I just could not take the chance that my mom would pack a peach in my lunch again and then, while I was secretly trying to throw it in the trash, Pinsetti or Angeline would spot it and cause a big Nickname Event. Then I'd have to run away from home.
   And just to prove that the entire Universe is on the side of evil, perfect Angeline, it was Meat Loaf Day in the cafeteria. Thursday is always Meat Loaf Day. The Cafeteria Monitor, Miss Bruntford, takes it personally when you don't eat something. And she gives us all kinds of grief, in particular when we don't eat the greasy cafeteria meat loaf.

Note supernatural resemblance of Bruntford to meat loaf

Miss Bruntford starts going, "What's wrong with the meat loaf?" and her giant slab of neck flubber starts waggling all over the place. She has one of those big, jiggly necks that looks like it might be soft and fluffy like the meringue on top of a lemon meringue pie.

So I had no choice but to eat some of the meat loaf, which smells a little like a wet cat, and that is Angeline's fault, too, as is everything.

Poke

One time a kid touched her NECK-FLUB AND DOCTORS DECLARED Him MEDICALLY GROSSED-OUT.

Friday 06

Dear Dumb Diary,

I don't know if I've ever mentioned Angeline before, but she's this girl at my school who is beautiful and popular and has hair the color of spun gold as if anybody likes that color.

Isabella and I were in the hallway today, and Isabella insanely tried to engage Angeline in conversation as she walked by, which was way out of line for Isabella since Angeline is like a "9" in popularity while Isabella is hovering around an unsteady "5." (And after Isabella's lip balm-dependent lips start decaying from Lip Smacker withdrawal, who knows how low that number could go?)

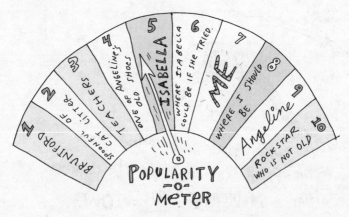

Anyway, Angeline just kind of looks at Isabella as if she's something peculiar and mildly gross like an inside-out nostril, and without saying a word, Angeline just keeps walking.

ISABELLA

Have you **EVER** known somebody like Angeline, Diary? Like maybe at the store where I bought you, there was some other really expensive diary that thought it was so cool that it walked around the store looking like it had a pen stuck up its binding?

Honestly, Dear Dumb Diary, if there **WAS** a diary like Angeline at the store, and you told me about it, I would go straight to the store and buy it and use its pages to pick up Stinker's you-know-whats when I take him for a walk. But also I would remind you to be happy with who you are, because you are beautiful and especially to be happy with your own hair, even though you don't have hair. But, you know, if you did and if it was real ugly.

ALSO GOOD idea

Goat EATING STUCK-UP DIARY

Isabella later told me that she thought she actually might be able to persuade Angeline to abandon ChocoMint. Isabella is a nice girl and I really like her, but if brains were bananas, let's just say that there would be a lot of skinny monkeys scraping around the inside of Isabella's skull.

Einstein's   Isabella's

DOES YOUR SKULL MONKEY LOOK AS BAD IN A BIKINI AS IT SHOULD?

PS: Nickname Update: Nobody has called me Peach Girl . . . *YET*. Angeline must be waiting for just the right time to spring it on me. It is a **KNOWN SCIENTIFIC FACT** that girls who are all pretty and Pure Goodness on the outside are Pure Evil inside.

Angeline is probably just waiting for the exact most embarrassing moment to unveil the Peach Girl nickname to the world.

true person

Saturday 07

Dear Dumb Diary,

Okay, okay. I know what I wrote yesterday about being happy with your own hair color. Maybe I was trying to be open-minded about accepting people with perfect blond hair, or maybe I was trying to be a scientist or something, but today I decided to buy one of those hair dye kits you can use at home. (You probably have never noticed, Dumb Diary, but the truth is: I have some hair issues.)

I picked the one that looked like Angeline's hair color, which they call "Glorious Heavenly Sunshine." I was not trying to copy Angeline, it just happened to be the first one I grabbed in the fourth store I looked.

I probably should have asked Isabella to help me with the hair dye but I didn't really want to get a lecture from her about self-acceptance while I pretended not to notice she was afflicted with a rapidly advancing case of what doctors call, "Lizard Lips."

I just locked myself in the bathroom and dyed alone.

SCIENCE

A MEDICAL STUDY OF LIZARD LIPS

STAGE 1

STAGE 2

STAGE 3

STAGE 4
(30 DAYS LATER)

(Which reminds me: I know why they call it "dye." Because after you see what it does, that's what you'll want to do.)

What was supposed to come out as "Glorious Heavenly Sunshine" came out the exact color of raw chicken. I could have hidden in the poultry case at the supermarket and been perfectly camouflaged.

So now I had to go back to the store and get a kit that would dye my hair back to its original color before Isabella or my mom could get on my case for not loving myself.

I pulled a clump of my old hair out of my brush so I could match it at the store, which didn't really strike me as gross until I saw how the clerk reacted when I handed it to her to help me find the right color. Luckily, they had the correct shade, and I brought it home and dyed my hair back.

By the way, you know how the name for Angeline's hair color is "Glorious Heavenly Sunshine"? The people at the dye company named the one that matches mine "Groundhog."

Sunday 08

Dear Dumb Diary,

Isabella came over much too early today (I was so glad that my hair was back the way that nature had inflicted).

She came over so early, in fact, that she actually saw my dad in his ugly plaid bathrobe that she said looks like he stole it off a homeless zombie, but I think looks **way** worse.

Anyway, Isabella just completed her Loser Scale, which identifies how much of a Loser somebody is, and therefore is a useful guide by which Loser-ness can be measured.

Isabella says that this is how the metric system started: that somebody just like her woke up one day and decided that a liter was a liter and pretty soon everybody agreed (even though nobody knows how much a liter actually is).

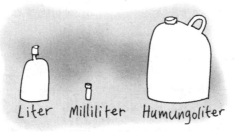

Liter   Milliliter   Humungoliter

Isabella will probably be a Professor of Popularity Science one day.

Here is Isabella's Metric System of Dorkology:

ISABELLA'S
LOSER SCALE
FROM BAD TO WORSE

DINK — PESTY, PARTIALLY STINKY

DORK — LOUD, OFTEN OAFISH.

DORKBAG — SPITTY-MOUTHED. LIKES TO LIE. TWITCHY.

TURD — MEAN AND THICK-HEADED. QUESTIONABLE SHOE CHOICES.

BLONDWAD — STEALER OF BALM FLAVORS. POSSIBLY UNFAMILIAR WITH SOAP.

TURDPIE — BIG-TIME ANNOYING. FUTURE CANNIBAL. UNFLATTERING WARDROBE.

Sunday 08 (late-breaking news)

Dear Dumb Diary,

After Isabella finished making me study her Dorkology System, I talked her into going up to the store to try to choose a new lip balm flavor. (She SO did not want to do it, but I made her. This sort of Gentle Pressure is part of the grieving process when somebody loses a loved one such as ChocoMint flavoring.)

Even though Isabella made me stand there forever while she rejected about forty perfectly good lip treatments, I had to tell her that the jumbo lip gloss she finally selected and liked was actually a roll-on deodorant.

So the effort was a huge failure, but I'm sorry: Friends tell friends they're wearing antiperspirants on their mouths.

EVEN GROSSER THAN it SOUNDS

Monday 09

Dear Dumb Diary,

School was okay today. Actually, it was *better* than okay. Angeline got her long, beautiful hair tangled in one of the jillion things she has dangling from her backpack and the school nurse — who is now one of my main heroes — took a pair of scissors and snipped two feet of silky blond hair from the left side of her head, so now Angeline only looks like The Prettiest Girl in the World if you're standing on her right. (Although personally, I think she would look better if I was standing on her neck.)

Also, I got an assignment in English class to do a report on mythology. I asked my teacher Mr. Evans what "mythology" meant exactly, and he said it's about things that don't exist. I asked if that would include the hair on the left side of Angeline's head, which got a pretty good laugh from everyone except Mr. Evans and Angeline.

Mr. Evans said that I pretty much need an A on my mythology report or my grades would be with the mermaids. "You know," he said, "Below C level."

Pretty funny, huh? I hope beautiful silky, blond hair grows on his big shiny bald head so that the nurse can cut half of it off.

Tuesday 10

Dear Dumb Diary,

How weird am I?

I had to go down to the school nurse today because I think Mom may have accidentally poisoned me with some sort of mushy noodley stuff we had with dinner last night that tasted almost exactly like socks smell.

I was hoping the nurse could give me some medicine or something, but she couldn't. She just had me lie quietly on a little cot for a while. Evidently, this is how they taught her to unpoison people.

me dying

It was pretty boring, of course, just lying there trying my hardest not to be poisoned, and I started looking around. And that's when I saw it in the wastebasket: A huge clump of long, beautiful blond hair. **Angeline's** hair.

And here's the weird part: I took it. I don't know why I took it — it's not like I know how to do voodoo against her or anything.

Yet.

I just wanted it.

me escaping with clump

And in case you're worried, Dumb Diary, it turns out I wasn't poisoned after all. The nurse said I probably just had a little "dyspepsia," which I think is the medical way to say that I had a humongous, gigantic amount of gas that could choke a horse.

Wednesday 11

Dear Dumb Diary,

I tried to figure out something to do with Angeline's hair clump today. There's not quite enough to make a decent wig. I thought about planting it like a bush to see if it would grow and grow until I had actually grown another Angeline head. But then I worried it might be more beautiful than the real first head, so forget that.

I guess for now I'll just keep it like a trophy, kind of like you might keep a moose's head on the wall, except that in this case I only got a wad of the moose's hair.

On the subject of her head, Angeline was wearing a little beret on it today to cover up her butchered haircut. (*Beret* is French for stupid hat). Anyway, nobody could believe how totally goony it looked. I'm sure this will be the end for her and Hudson.

31

Thursday 12

Dear Dumb Diary,

Like, half the people at school were wearing berets today (including **Hudson**!!!). It's like they were all secret beret-owners, just waiting for a signal from Angeline that it was okay to start wearing their berets. I don't understand it. What if Angeline had accidentally worn her underpants on her head? I think we all know *exactly* what would have happened. Half the school would have been walking around peeking out the leg holes of their boxers.

IDIOT   BUFFOON   half-
                        wit

There are only two things about this that really bug me:

1) People only like Angeline because she is totally beautiful and nice and smart.

2) I don't have a beret.

It was Meat Loaf Day again today, like it is every Thursday. The Cafeteria Monitor, Miss Bruntford, made a big deal (again) about the uneaten meat loaf, but the kids who were wearing their dumb berets were all kind of unified, like the French Resistance, and they just ignored her. This made her even madder, and I noticed that she waggled her neck blubber extra furiously at Angeline, as if she knew that the berets were all Angeline's fault.

WAGGLE WAGGLE WAGGLE

Intense Neck Vibrations actually Register As MILD EARTHQUAKE Six miles AWAY

SEISMOGRAPH

Food-Crime Update: Mom made something for dinner that was so bad, I decided to chance the lecture on Wheretheheckistan and sneak it to Stinker, my beagle. Stinker tried a bite and then, to get the taste out of his mouth, went and ate half of the grit in the cat box.

Now I am a little bit afraid of Stinker, who I think might blame me for how sick he got later, although it was totally Mom's fault and if he is planning on biting somebody's neck while they sleep, it should not be mine. (Dumb Diary, I am saying this out loud as I write so that Stinker can hear me.)

vengeful beagle

Friday 13

Dear Dumb Diary,

It's only about one week until my cousin gets here and Mom and Dad are on **FULL CHILD SAFETY** alert.

They've been putting special indestructible childproof latches on the cabinets where we keep cleaning products and bug killers because, evidentially, little children like to eat them.

Seems like a lot of work. If we don't want kids to eat those things, wouldn't it be simpler to just make them broccoli flavored?

Saturday 14

Dear Dumb Diary,

    I figured that I had better do something to prepare for the mythology thing in Mr. Evans's class.

    I went online and read about Medusa, who had poisonous snakes growing out of her head, and who would have been totally jealous of a girl with real hair even if it was the color of a groundhog.

    I have one piece of advice for people with poisonous vipers for hair: Ponytails. Bangs. Something.

BEFORE MAKEOVER

WORN UP IN PROM STYLE

BRAIDS

GLAMOROUS WAVE

I also read about Icarus who made wings out of wax and then flew too close to the sun and they melted. The moral is this: If Icarus had been meant to fly, he would have been born a flight attendant like my cousin Terrence.

Did you know, Dumb Diary, that mythology can include things like trolls and giants and talking fish since it wasn't just the Greeks and Romans that had mythology? Old Dead Guys everywhere had mythology, which I think is very, very interesting to somebody somewhere, maybe.

Finding sunglasses that look cool is the WORST PART of BEING A CYCLOPS

Saturday 14 (late-breaking news)

Dear Dumb Diary,

Isabella and I were out walking this afternoon and we accidentally walked about a half mile out of our way and *accidentally* found ourselves way over by Derby Street, which was a peculiar coincidence because that is sort of near where Hudson Rivers lives exactly.

Isabella said that walking past his house like this was a form of stalking, but I told her that it wasn't because stalkers are crazy, and we were sane enough to wear disguises.

 flawless disguise

The disguises turned out to be a pretty good idea because as we walked past, Hudson happened to look out the window, which freaked out Isabella who ran — but not before she pushed me down on the lawn.

I caught up to her six blocks later. She apologized, explaining that she only pushed me down before running because of what was probably just an instinct, like if a bear was chasing us.

Since it was only that, I forgave her.

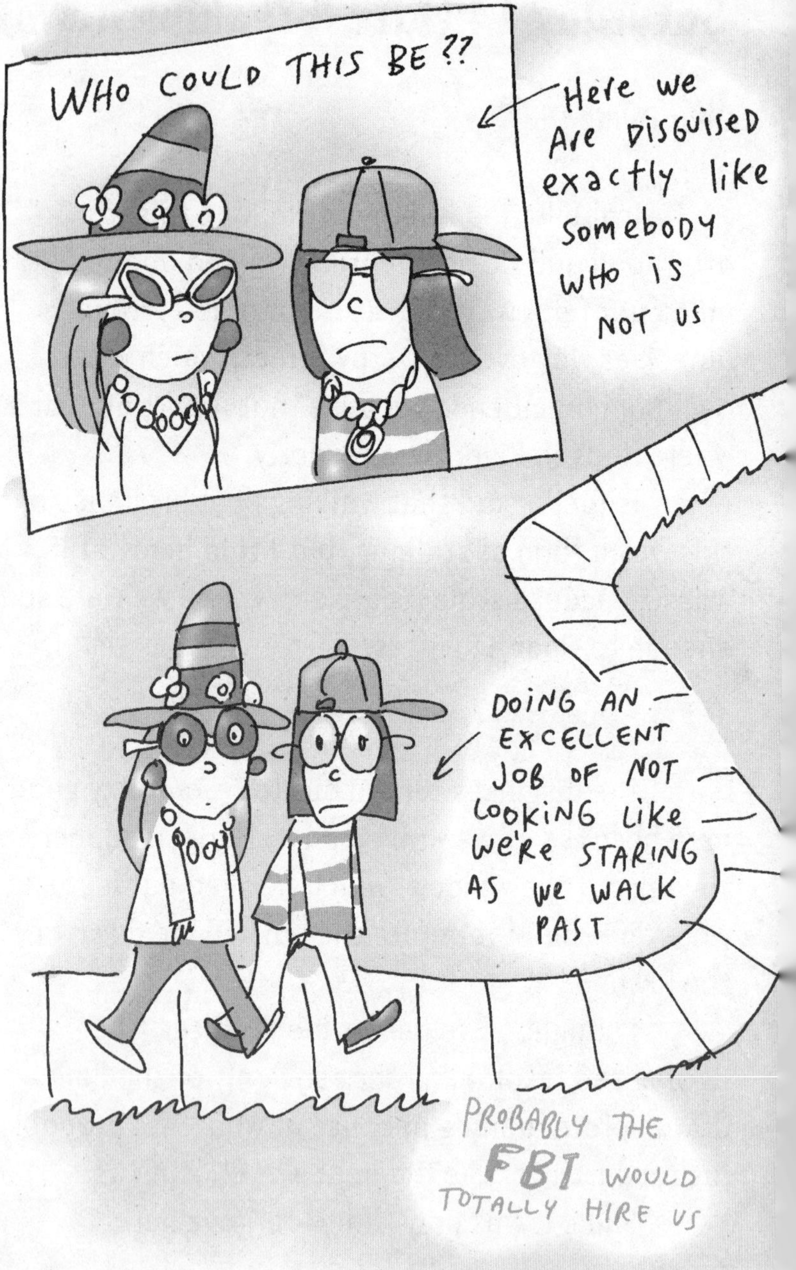
WHO COULD THIS BE??
Here we Are Disguised exactly like somebody who is NOT US
DOING AN EXCELLENT JOB OF NOT LOOKING LIKE WE'RE STARING AS WE WALK PAST
PROBABLY THE FBI WOULD TOTALLY HIRE US

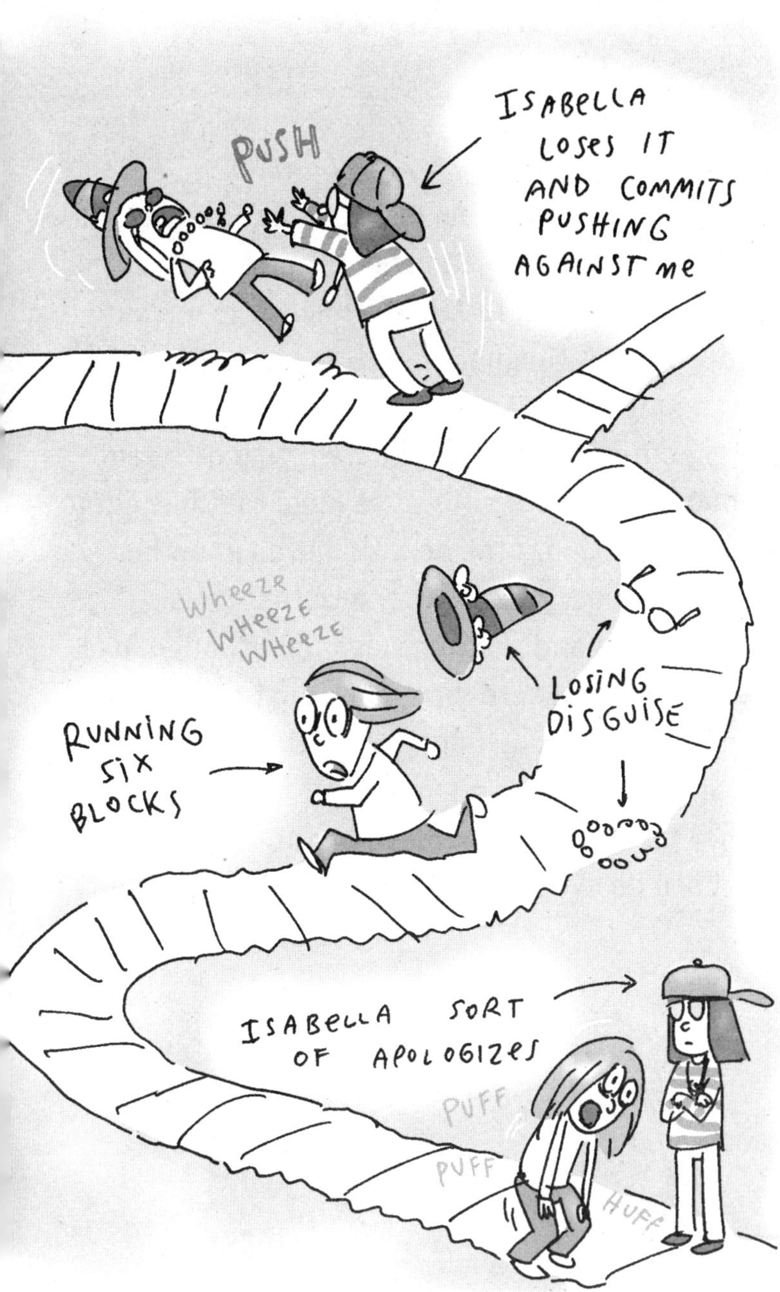
ISABELLA LOSES IT AND COMMITS PUSHING AGAINST ME
PUSH
WHEEZE WHEEZE WHEEZE
RUNNING SIX BLOCKS
LOSING DISGUISE
ISABELLA SORT OF APOLOGIZES
PUFF
PUFF
HUFF

Sunday 15

Dear Dumb Diary,

I finally found a beret at the mall. It cost me thirty bucks, which wiped me out, and I don't even like it, but a fad is a fad, and frankly, I'm not sure if I'm cool enough to ignore a fad. It's a very difficult thing to judge.

I heard about a girl who went to a different school and tried to ignore some huge fad, like cargo pants or something. The next thing you know her family forced her to marry her own first cousin once-removed and she went insane. Although, as I write this, I'm not sure if that has anything to do with cargo pants, and I don't even think the government lets people marry their first cousins whether they are once-removed or not. It's all probably a lie except the cargo pants and insane parts.

AAAARAA AA

me insane

Anyway, I'm tired and it's time for bed. I'm going to try to force myself to dream that a huge toad gobbles up Angeline and then the toad is eaten by a giant hog and then the hog is made into this awful toad-flavored ham that is served at Angeline's sixteenth birthday party and everybody gets sick including Angeline who is somehow magically alive again to eat her own ghastly toad-hog-ham self.

I don't always remember my dreams but I'll know if I dream this one because I'll wake up laughing so hard my stomach will hurt.

isn't imagination a lovely thing?

Monday 16

Dear Dumb Diary,

The beret fad is over. As I threw my *thirty-dollar* beret in the trash, I wondered how could it be over so fast. Do you wonder, too, Dumb Diary? Well, stay tuned . . .

Today in science, Mr. Tweeds gave us an out-loud pop quiz where he asked everybody one question. This was the question he gave me:

"How could you determine which way north is using only a needle?"

Here is what I answered: "Find a smart person and threaten to stick it in him if he won't tell you which way north is."

Which I guess I knew was wrong, but didn't realize it was wrong enough to get you sent to the principal's office.

And by the way, Diary, here's an easy way to remember if you spell it princi**ple** or princi**pal**. (Maybe you've heard it before, Diary?) Just remember that **pal**eontology is the study of fossils that are about a *jillion* years old.

PALeONTOLOGY   PRINCIPAL

Oh. And by the way: I have solved *The Mystery of the Sudden Demise of the Beret Fad*. On my way to the principal's office I saw that all of the secretary women in the school office were wearing berets.

Thanks a lot, ladies. Maybe next time I'll take a chance on marrying cousin Terrence.

Now get this, **Dumb Diary:** While I was in his office, the principal pulled out the folder containing my permanent record to make a note of this latest smartmouthery. (As you know, your permanent record follows you through school and is not destroyed until you are married or dead or something.) But when he pulled out my folder, I noticed, just a couple folders away from mine . . . ANGELINE'S PERMANENT RECORD.

I WAS MILDLY INTERESTED

Instantly, I knew I had a goal in life: To possess and share the horrible contents of this folder with the world, and to reveal to mankind the boyfriend/scent thief that Angeline really is.

Oops. I got so excited on that last part that I dropped my diary on Stinker's head, who was asleep. And I think he might be swearing in dog language right now.

Tuesday 17

Dear Dumb Diary,

I tried to think about doing something on my mythology report today, since it's getting close to the deadline, and it's probably time to actually make some progress regarding starting to worry about it. I want to work on it, really and truly I do, but I think I may have caught a little case of **OCD** about Angeline's permanent record.

evil SPIRIT oF ANGELiNE's FOLDeR ↘

← me innocently trying to do my homework

OCD, in case you've never heard of it, Dumb Diary, stands for Obsessive-Compulsive Disorder, and it's this condition where you become obsessive and compulsive about things. It makes you think about something so much that you do things like wash your hands a hundred times a day, or open your locker over and over to make sure you haven't forgotten anything for your next class, or keep saying over and over to yourself "I must have Angeline's permanent record."

Anyway, since it's psychological, and not from germs, I'm pretty sure you can catch it from watching a talk show about it, which is how I think I may have caught it. Obviously, Mom will be calling me in sick tomorrow morning.

DISEASES YOU CAN CATCH FROM WATCHING T.V.

THINKING A MANIAC IS HIDING IN YOUR CLOSET

OCD

TALKING WITH DUMB ACCENT

KNOWLEDGE THAT THERE ARE A JILLION BRANDS OF CAT LITTER

WORRYING THAT THE MARK ON YOUR ARM IS A LITTLE BIT OF PLAGUE

Oh. And one other thing: Angeline's bald hair patch is almost totally invisible now. She has employed some sort of secret military combing technology to camouflage the patch she had been covering with the beret. It is also possible that she simply regenerated the lost hair, regrowing it the way a lizard regrows a lost tail or a slug regrows — I don't know — a big snotty lump or something that somebody cuts off him.

ANGELINE'S FREAKISH HEAD

BEFORE

AFTER

SINISTER MILITARY SECRET
OR
EVIDENCE OF SUBHUMAN PARENTS?
You decide!

Wednesday 18

Dear Dumb Diary,

Mom would not call me in sick from school today. But it's okay, because I have miraculously recovered from my **OCD** and actually do not even think about or care about Angeline anymore. Let me prove it. Below, I will write the names of people that I just don't care about at all.

George Washington, Ringo Starr, Christina Aguilera, Zeus, Angeline, Dan Rather, Caesar Riley, Angeline, Paul Bunyan, Cleopatra, Nefertiti, Maria Barbo, Angeline, Koko the Signing Gorilla, The Yellow Teletubby, Angeline, Angeline, Angeline, Angeline, ANGELINE

Thursday 19

Dear Dumb Diary,

Okay, okay. Maybe Angeline does still bug me a little. I just *had* to have Angeline's permanent record, and the only way to do it was to get sent to the principal's office again.

So at lunch today, Miss Bruntford, the neck-waggling cafeteria monitor, lost her mind and said that nobody could leave the cafeteria until they had finished the meat loaf. She was staring at us and we were staring at her and you could have cut the tension with a knife, which is something you can't do with the meat loaf.

SCHOOL IS AN ENDLESS BATTLE BETWEEN the forces of GOOD AND THE FAT-NECKED FORCES OF EVIL

Suddenly, a big honkin' slab of the shiny slippery meat loaf came flying through the air and smacked Miss Bruntford right in the neck blubber.

She started screaming and sputtering and demanding to know who did it. It seemed like a golden opportunity, so I said that I was the one who had thrown it. Easy ticket to the principal's office, right?

SPLOT

Boxer
ShoRTS?
I suspect so.

But get this: As they're hustling me out of the cafeteria like I'm a perp on that *COPS* show, I'm looking down at everybody's trays. I see meat loaf after meat loaf after meat loaf. And then I see one tray without meat loaf. I look up, and there's Angeline, wiping gravy off her hand with a napkin.

ANGELINE!!! She was the one that threw the meat loaf, and I had taken the fall for it.

The GRAVY OF GUILT

Of course, I got a big lecture from the principal and he might have even mentioned Wheretheheckistan. Plus, he banned me from eating school lunches for two weeks. (I got the feeling that he thought that was a much worse punishment than it actually was.)

And, to make things worse, of course I did not get Angeline's permanent record. (I mean, what did I think I was going to do? Knock the principal out with a karate kick and just grab the folder out of the file cabinet???) It turns out this was a pretty lousy idea. I'm never going to try something that dumb again.

Even if you are justified like I am kicking a PRINCIPAL's HEAD OFF is STILL NOT ENTIRELY Right.

Friday 20

Dear Dumb Diary,

I tried something that dumb again. Between classes, I saw the principal talking to Miss Anderson who is a teacher and therefore old, but is beautiful enough to be a waitress, and all the men teachers talk to her for a long time. I ran all the way to the office and walked right in and asked to talk to the principal. He wasn't there, so one of the secretaries told me to come back later, but I told her I had a private matter to discuss with him, and could I leave him a note? Then I told her that with that beret on, I thought for a second she was one of the school cheerleaders.

She ACTUALLY Believed it.

Of course, she let me right in and all I had to do was just walk over to the cabinet and snatch Angeline's permanent record. I know what you're thinking, Dumb Diary: You are thinking that I am the Smartest Chick in the World. And you're right. I *am* the Smartest Chick in the World.

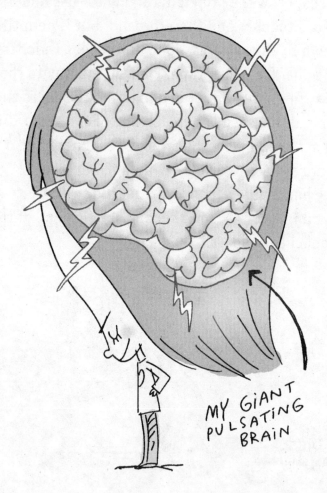

MY GIANT PULSATING BRAIN

And later on, the Smartest Chick in the World forgot Angeline's file at school. On a *Friday*. So now I'll have **OCD** about it all weekend.

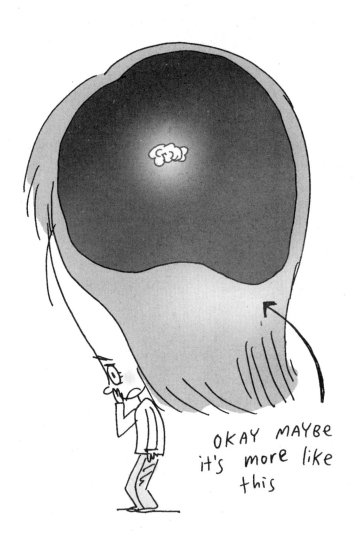

OKAY MAYBe it's more like this

Saturday 21

Dear Dumb Diary,

What's the name of that little animal with the big head and the sharp little teeth? Oh yeah: Eddy. My aunt dropped off Cousin Eddy today with his permanently sticky face and Robot Avenger backpack. She had a big long list of things he liked and things he didn't, but most of all, she said, don't give him anything with strawberries in it because he's allergic.

Mom keeps washing his face, but, like, three minutes later he's sticky again. He's like a doughnut that secretes its own glaze. Mom yelled at me for using my finger to write "wash me" on his cheek.

Sunday 22

Dear Dumb Diary,

Angeline uses such a wonderful and important shampoo that the small wad of hair I have has actually made our whole house smell better. It also has a powerful effect on Eddy, who seems to have an unnatural love for it, and a mutant ability to sniff it out of its hiding places.

My Scientific Theory is that since Eddy will grow up into a Guy one day, he is already instinctively and unnaturally in love with Angeline. The hair has no effect on my dad, and Isabella says that is because he is my dad and stopped being a Guy when he met my mom.

The fragrance also seems to have an effect on Stinker, who sneezes and sneezes whenever I grind the hair wad in his face. I wonder if that annoys him?

SNARL GRRR GRR

ZOMBIE-LIKE DEVOTION TO HAIR WAD

Dear Dumb Diary,

There's good news and there's bad news. The good news is Mom says that my aunt is picking up Eddy on Thursday, which is a relief because I'm getting tired of trying to hide Angeline's hair wad from him. There's more good news. I remembered to bring Angeline's permanent record home. But I set it down one second and turned my back and when I reached for it again it was gone. I know it was either Stinker or Eddy who took it, but no amount of yelling or depriving of toys or dog bones has had any effect. And Eddy really likes those bones.

WHICH ONE IS GUILTY?

The mangy flea-bitten Animal or the dog?

Tuesday 24

Dear Dumb Diary,

It is making me mental that Angeline's permanent record is in this house and I cannot find it. I even looked in Stinker's doghouse, which meant I had to throw out all the sticks and trash he had been keeping in there. Since then, Stinker has been staring at me for hours with his black, black, dog eyes and I think he may be planning something against me.

Maybe I should buy a dozen big mean cats to have around the house in case some mean little dog shows up to try to do something mean to me. (Dumb Diary, I read that last sentence out loud so that Stinker could hear it, but it did not seem to have any effect on him. If I turn up missing in the morning, I just hope the police dust for fingerprints, or foot prints, or whatever you call the prints left by those paw-nubs on the bottom of a guilty beagle's foot. Hint, hint.)

BIG MEAN CAT

ARE YOU GETTING all this, Stinker?

Wednesday 25

Dear Dumb Diary,

I'm angry on the outside . . .

. . . but I'm far angrier on the inside.

I finally finished my mythology report. In spite of distractions, like cousin Eddy clawing at the door to get in, and the frustrating knowledge that there could be something so joyfully horrendous in Angeline's folder that it could be used to reduce her to a tiny quivering lump of sobbing goo, and I do not know where the folder is.

Happily, Mom told me that Eddy won't be here much longer — my aunt is meeting us at school tomorrow morning to pick him up.

I wonder if I'll miss having him around the house? I didn't miss Stinker's Frantic Itchy Butt Disease when that cleared up, so I think I'll be okay when Eddy is gone.

THE WORLD OF THE BEAGLE
DOES IT REVOLVE AROUND HIS BUTT?

Itches a little

Itches medium

Total freak-out
knock-a-table-over
itchiness

Asleep but it
still itches

65

Thursday 26

Dear Dumb Diary,

   Stinker ate my mythology report.
   I guess at least now I know what he's been planning. He was waiting for me to finish it. Here's how I know he was doing it to get back at me: He only ate the words. He left the paper margins in his bowl like pizza crusts.

I had to pack my own lunch this morning, on account of being banned from buying lunch at school. There was only a spoonful of strawberry jam for my sandwich and just to make things worse, Stinker must have licked it off my bread while I went to the fridge to look for a juice box. I figured he did it to get the taste of mythology out his mouth — which probably tastes awful — so I didn't even get that mad at him. My mom finished packing my lunch and stuck it in my backpack.

Mythology might taste worse than Mom's cooking

So there I was, Dumb Diary. Mom was dropping me off at school, and I knew I was headed for an "F" from Mr. Evans. I mean, you just can't actually *say* the dog ate your homework. I have to give that mean little beagle credit: Stinker played that one beautifully.

While I was headed into school, my aunt met my mom outside, and they were getting ready to transfer Eddy from one minivan to another when he escaped, I guess.

And the way I know that is because while I was walking the Walk of the Condemned toward Mr. Evans's class, a small, dirty savage went whipping past me in the halls with his little Robot Avenger backpack followed by my screaming aunt. I was just about to grab Eddy for her when I noticed Hudson walking past, and I had to quickly decide if I was going to help a family member or try to look cool for a guy that probably hardly knows I'm alive.

"Hi, Hudson," I said as Eddy scrambled out of sight around the corner followed by my aunt who I think was starting to cry.

I walked into Mr. Evans's class, knowing full well that I would be going first. Mr. Evans called on me to stand up in front of the class and give my presentation.

I had just started to say "Mr. Evans, I don't have my —" when Eddy ran into the class. His face was swollen and his tongue was so thick I couldn't understand whatever he was jabbering. I suddenly knew that Stinker had not licked my bread this morning — Eddy had. I guess he really *is* allergic to strawberries. Eddy was so puffy he looked like a picture of himself somebody had drawn on a balloon.

Before   After

Eddy saw my backpack at the same time I saw him use his supernatural hair-wad-locating-ability against me, and we both lunged for it. But the little demon-child was faster, and he managed to get his big round head inside the backpack before I could stop him. When I finally pulled his head out, he had Angeline's hair clump stuck like a beard to his always-sticky face. With his dirty clothes and beard and weird swollen-faced jabbering, he didn't seem human.

The fact that I was holding Eddie around his neck as he kicked and growled and clawed at the air did not do much to create the impression that he was a human being, either.

Mr. Evans jumped to his feet and turned red and started bulging his forehead vein at us and was all "Do you know this . . . child, Jamie?" That's when I realized that the next thing out of my mouth was going to get me failed, and also nicknamed throughout the school as the Girl with the Crazy Cousin, or something worse: Mike Pinsetti was quickly jotting down a few nickname ideas on a sheet of paper. You could tell he was trying out a few things. I thought about pitching Eddy out the second-story window.

Then, it happened. Eddy had knocked my lunch bag out of my backpack, and what comes rolling out and stops right in front of me? A **PEACH.** My mom had packed a *peach.*

Angeline stood up. This was it. This was her big opportunity. She had waited for just the right moment, and this was obviously IT.

Angeline walked to the front of the class, and stood next to me. She smiled her perfect Angeline smile and said, "Mr. Evans, Jamie and I did our report together. We did it on trolls. And this," she said, pointing to Eddy, "is our visual aid."

She didn't call me Peach Girl. She didn't do anything bad. Angeline was **ACTUALLY HELPING ME**. Mr. Evans and the whole class — even Hudson — suddenly looked like they were getting this giant backrub from Angeline's voice, which is the most beautiful mortal voice ever heard, but so what?

people melted into puddle of sick love for ANGELINE

My butt was on the line here. So, I went with it. The two of us started making it up as we went along and every time Eddy would snarl or growl the whole class would laugh, and I think Eddy even started to like it. I quickly realized this was the best report I had ever given, and I was actually enjoying giving it. Just as we finished, my aunt showed up at the door and took Eddy away, and we got an A on the report and even a round of applause. (Isabella had to do her best not to smile. Her lips are so dry now that even a slight smile will split them open like a pair of burnt hot dogs.)

As I went back to my desk, I asked myself: **Why would Angeline help me out?** Could it have been because I took the fall for her meat loaf crime? Were we supposed to be friends now? The thought of it just made me totally ill. I looked **SO** sick, in fact, that Mr. Evans told me to get my stuff and go down to the school nurse.

How could EVANS tell that I felt sick?

When I went for my bag, I saw Eddy's Robot Avenger backpack on the floor next to it, and peeking out of just one little corner, I saw Angeline's permanent record. I scooped it up and headed for the nurse's office.

How I tried to Look

How I probably Looked

The nurse did what she always does. It doesn't matter if you have a heart attack, a leg eaten off by bear, or an ax stuck in your face, it's always the same thing: **Lie Down on the Cot and Rest.**

ILLNESSES OUR NURSE TRIES TO CURE WITH THE COT

HEADACHE

SWALLOWED BY PYTHON

RACCOON MISHAP

NOTHING LEFT BUT SKELETON

While I was lying there, I looked at the cover of Angeline's permanent record. Before I opened it, I amused myself with what might be inside: Maybe counterfeiting, kidnapping, fixing the outcome of school football games by means of insincere eyelash-batting at quarterbacks.

Or maybe she had been brought up on charges of spending her whole life as somebody who people can't help but like even though deep down they really and truly want to hate her.

All that was left to do was open it, and read it, and then share its terrible contents with the World.

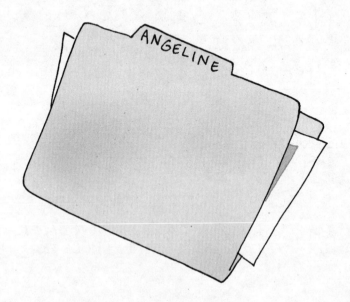

Friday 27

Dear Dumb Diary,

Angeline sat down across from Isabella and me at lunch today. I was eating a ham-and-cheese sandwich that I had packed for lunch but we were all out of cheese, and I had felt guilty about how I had treated Stinker so I had given him the last slice of ham as a truce. I guess you would call it a mustard sandwich if I had remembered to put mustard on it.

Who Doesn't enjoy a nice nothing sandwich?

(By the way, Stinker and I are pals again. I guess he figured that eating my homework had made us even for the last couple of weeks. Thinking back, I suppose that **WAS** fair.)

Okay, back to Angeline (remember Angeline?). Incredibly, between bites of bread, I actually said this to Angeline: "Thanks for saving my life on the report yesterday." I didn't actually intend to be polite. I've been brainwashed by my parents to be polite against my will sometimes.

Then she smiled at me. And it wasn't totally an Aren't-I-Great-with-My-Perfect-Teeth-and-Gums-Smile. It was a regular smile. And she said, "We should do something sometime. A movie or something. Maybe you can teach me how to do that thing you do with your hair," she said, pointing at my head. "I can never get my hair to do anything cool."

CONFUSINGLY NON-EVIL

And the very next thing I knew, Dumb Diary, Miss Bruntford, the Cafeteria Monitor had me in a Heimlich position and was trying to disgorge a bread chunk that I had accidentally inhaled when Angeline had complimented my hair. After a couple squeezes, up it came, and I saw Mike Pinsetti standing there, grinning. It was obvious that he had crafted some excellent nickname for me that he was about to unveil, and everybody was waiting to hear what it was going to be, when Angeline grabbed him by the collar and said, "Just don't, **PIN-HEADY**."

SQUISH

CHOKING CAN KILL YOU.

HUMILIATION CAN ALMOST MAKE YOU WISH IT HAD.

OINK

SPLAT

PIN-HEADY. It was a masterpiece of nicknaming. It rhymed with his real name, it was insulting, and everybody in the cafeteria was standing there to hear it used for the first time. Even though he was utterly shattered, you could see a reluctant respect on Mike's face.

Angeline, who no one even knew had any cruelty within her at all, had shown the meanness that Isabella and I had always known was there.

TRUTH

I sure hope people DON'T WORSHIP me TOO MUCH FOR REVEALING THE TRUTH

Sure, she had only been cruel to Pin-heady (look how I am already forgetting his real name) and, yes, she kind of saved my neck again by not letting him get off a nickname for me, but c'mon, at least the world now knew that she's not this total perfect angel.

I know what you're thinking, Dumb Diary:
Use the old one-two punch. I have her permanent
record to share with the World. I can fix her once
and for all.

Except that I *don't* have it anymore.
Yesterday I had decided not to read Angeline's permanent record. I just slipped out of the nurse's office and into the principal's office and put it back in the file cabinet.

Besides, I thought, this is Angeline, how bad could it have **REALLY** been?

Isabella's lips cleared up a couple hours after lunch. It was like a miracle. They turned from what looked like sad little splintered slivers of beef jerky into what looks like full, ripe luscious crescents of papaya.

It was the meat loaf. The mysterious meat it's made from had some sort of incredible healing power on Isabella's lips. And it's her new signature flavor. She stuffed a wad of it into an old lip-balm tube. I know. It's awful. But it smells better than ChocoMint.

But that was only the second weirdest thing that the Universe did today.

Later on, after school, Angeline walked right up to me.

"I forgot to say thanks," she said.

"For what?" I said.

"For taking the blame for my meat loafing of the monitor."

And then, when she said that, IT *happened.* I felt the entire Universe groan and creak and shift slightly, and the next thing I knew, her terrible Angeline powers were starting to work on me. I felt as though I might be starting to LIKE ANGELINE AGAINST MY WILL.

I told Angeline it was no big deal. I had always wanted to do that myself.

"No, no. It **was** a big deal," she said. "You have no idea how much trouble I would have gotten in. If you could see what my permanent record looks like, you'd know. One more incident, and I'd be out of here and you'd have Hudson all to yourself, and I am **NOT** going to let that happen." Then she smiled and walked away.

I stood there for a while, Dumb Diary, sort of like a black-eyed beagle who has just seen all of his most precious sticks and trash thrown out by someone who has mistaken him for someone he is not. I was frozen in my spot by feelings of affection and hatred all glopped together like one of Mom's inedible Food-Crimes.

Maybe people are like meat loaf: Strong medicine, but also deadly poison.

I wondered, as Mike Pinsetti walked by me without making eye contact, if I could find the wisdom that Stinker had found and could exact the precise amount of justice called for here, which was to simply eat Angeline's homework sometime, and then call it even.

WELL, IT'S STILL PROBABLY BETTER THAN MOM'S COOKING.

Thanks for listening, Dumb Diary.

Jamie Kelly

Think you can handle another Jamie Kelly diary? Then check out

Dear Dumb Diary,

Anyway, Isabella said it wasn't the makeover that boosted Margaret's popularity and forced us down. **It was the pants.** She said it wasn't my loud "yahoo" in science that got me switched again so that I'm science partners with Known Goon, Mike Pinsetti. **It was the pants.** And she said it wasn't me that had done you-know-what all over Hudson Rivers. **It was the pants!**

Can't get enough of Jamie Kelly?
Check out her other Dear Dumb Diary books!

#1 LET'S PRETEND
THIS NEVER HAPPENED

#2 MY PANTS
ARE HAUNTED!

#3 AM I THE PRINCESS
OR THE FROG?

#4 NEVER DO
ANYTHING, EVER

#5 CAN ADULTS
BECOME HUMAN?

#6 THE PROBLEM
WITH HERE IS THAT IT'S
WHERE I'M FROM

#7 NEVER
UNDERESTIMATE
YOUR DUMBNESS

#5 IT'S NOT MY FAULT
I KNOW EVERYTHING

OUR DUMB DIARY:
A JOURNAL TO SHARE
WHERE I'M FROM

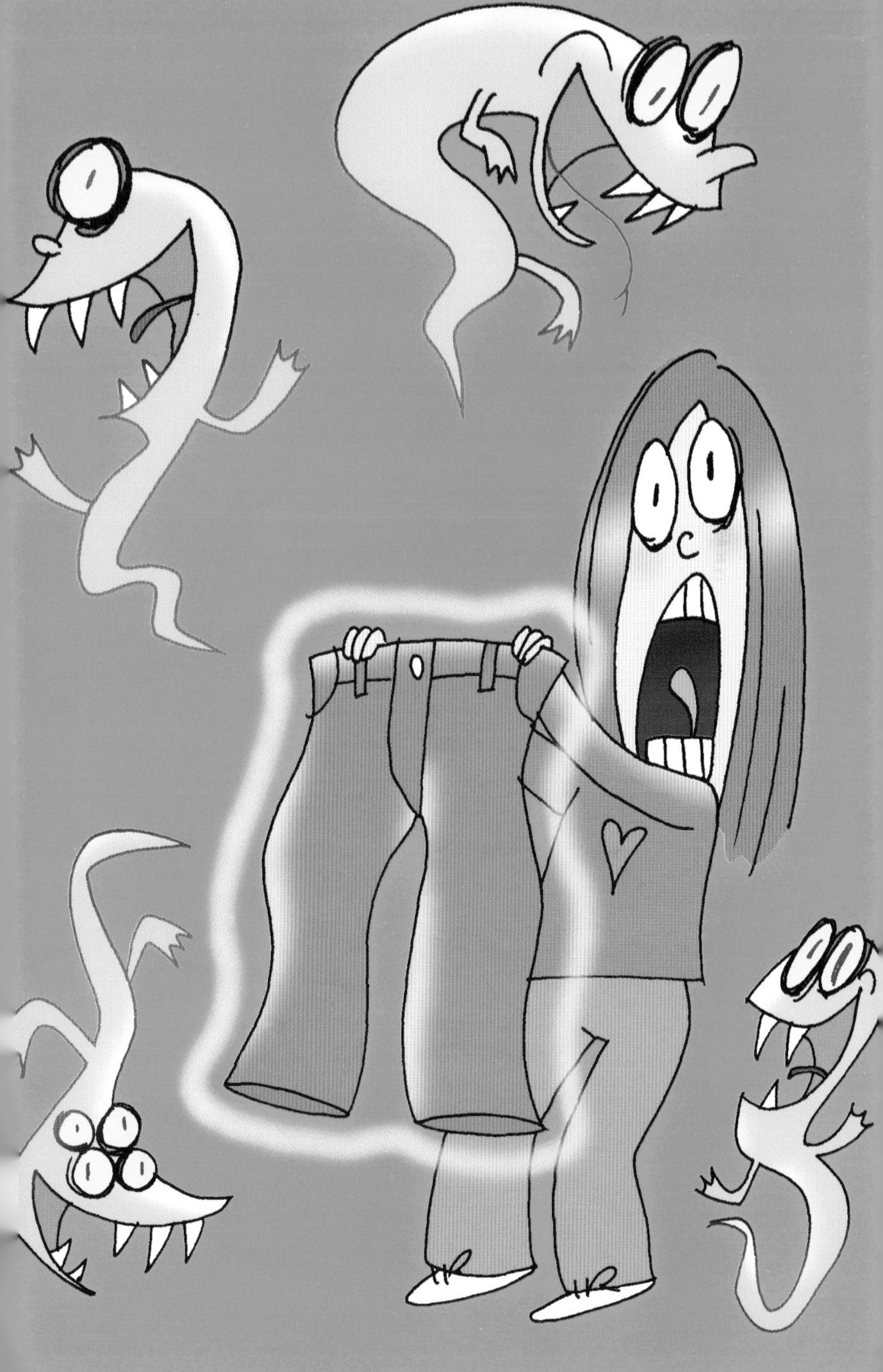

MY PANTS
ARE HAUNTED!

Think you can handle another Jamie Kelly diary?

DEAR DUMB DIARY,

MY PANTS ARE HAUNTED!

BY JAMIE KELLY

SCHOLASTIC INC.

New York   Toronto   London   Auckland   Sydney
Mexico City   New Delhi   Hong Kong   Buenos Aires

ISBN-13: 978-0-439-62905-8
ISBN-10: 0-439-62905-5

21 20 19 18 17 16 15 14 13 12 11 10   9 10 11 12 13/0

Printed in China   40

First printing, October 2004

For
the misunderstood.

Special thanks to:
Julie Kane-Ritsch and Carole Postal
along with all the punks at Scholastic, including:
Martha Atwater, Maria Barbo, Steve Scott,
Susan Jeffers Casel, and Shannon Penney.

THIS DIARY PROPERTY OF

Jamie Kelly

SCHOOL: MACKEREL MIDDLE SCHOOL

Locker: 101

Best friend: Isabella

Pet: Stinker (beagle)

Occupation: FASHion expert and makeover guru

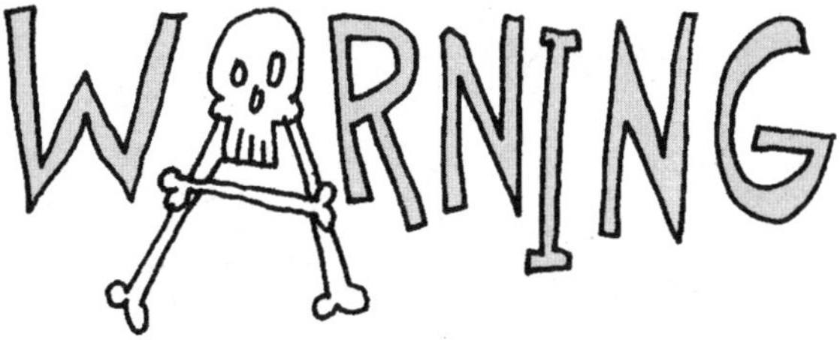
WARNING

READ NO FURTHER

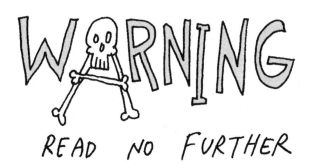

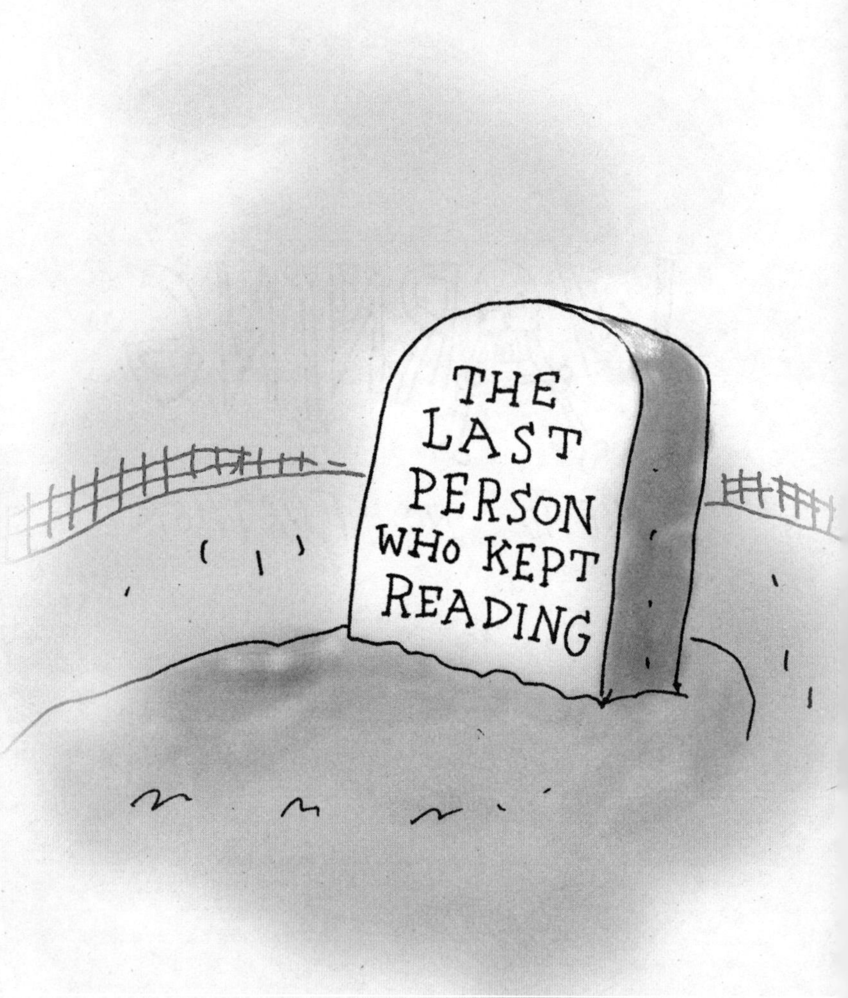
THE
LAST
PERSON
WHO KEPT
READING

UNLESS you are me,

I command you to stop reading now.

if you are me,
sorry, it's cool

Dear Whoever Is Reading My Dumb Diary,

Are you sure you're supposed to be reading somebody else's diary? Have you done this before? If I did not give YOU permission, YOU had better stop right now.

If you are my parents, then YES, I know that I am not allowed to call people idiots and fools and goons and half-wits and gerds and all that, but this is a diary, and I didn't actually "call" them anything. I *wrote* it. And if you punish me for it, then I will know that you read my diary, which I am *not* giving you permission to do.

Now, by the power vested in me, I do promise that everything in this diary is true, or at least as true as I think it needs to be.

Signed,

Jamie Kelly

PS: If this is you, Angeline, reading this, then you are officially busted. I happen to have this entire room under hidden video surveillance. And, in just a moment, little doors will slide open and flesh-eating rats will stream into the room. And, like tiny venomous cowboys, scorpions will be riding the rats. So it's curtains for you, Angeline! Mwah-hah-hah-hah!

PSS: If this is you, Margaret or Sally, then HA-HA — you are also caught in my surveillance sting.

PSSS: If this is you, Isabella, don't you ever get tired of reading my diary? I mean, I've caught you doing it, like, nine or ten times, so just STOP IT. Seriously. Maybe you should see somebody about this.

Dear Jamie-
I am <u>so</u> sure. I do <u>NOT</u> read your diary. So get over yourself.

         -Isabella

PS- I totally agree with the stuff you said about your mom.

Sunday 01

Dear Dumb Diary,

    Mom and I got into a "discussion" about fashion after dinner tonight. Of course, she really has no idea what the trends are at my school. I told her that I think she can't possibly know how important trends can be, and she said that clothes were just as important when she was in middle school. Then I said that I understood how she probably always tried her best to make a good impression on Fred and Wilma and Barney and the whole gang down at the tar pit, but times had changed.

a typical mother-daughter discussion

And that's just part of the reason I'm here in my room way ahead of schedule for the evening. Here's the exchange that followed my Mom-Is-Old-As-Cavemen joke:

"Just how do you think that makes me feel?" Mom asked.

"Stupid?" I guessed.

MOST DANGEROUS THINGS ON EARTH

BEAR THAT CAN BURP UP HAND GRENADES

GIANT SHARK WITH LITTLE SHARKS FOR TEETH

MY MOM WHEN YOU'RE TRYING TO MAKE HER ANGRY

Turns out that Mom had a different answer in mind, and I'll have a little time to figure out what it was since I'm here in my bedroom about five hours earlier than usual.

I also think that Dad sitting there trying *not* to laugh might have made things worse.

You can always tell when Dad is trying not to laugh

Sometimes diaries can be so much easier to talk to than moms. I can't picture Mom letting me write on her face, and I imagine sliding a bookmark in somewhere would result in a major wrestling match.

Monday 02

Dear Dumb Diary,

   Angeline is back to her old tricks, Dumb Diary.

   Yeah, sure, for a long time, everything was fine between us. (Nearly four whole days — except two of those were over the weekend, during which I did not see her.) But then today, in science class, while I was talking to Hudson Rivers (eighth cutest guy in my grade), she performed an act of **UTTER BEAUTY** and distracted him.

   Actually, I hadn't started to talk to him yet, but I was going to, and she should have known that when she whipped out her **GORGEOUSNESS** and waved it all over the place.

Isn't it time we stopped the beautiful people?

It's true. I may not be fully qualified to talk to Hudson Rivers. Maybe he *is* just slightly too cute for me. (I'm right on the edge of adorable.) But if I'm really, really lucky and keep my fingers crossed, he could become mildly disfigured. Then we'd be on the same level, and I want to make sure I'm ready should that blessed maiming occur.

SQUOOSH

A Beautiful thought
You are just one Rampaging Elephant away from marrying the Handsomest Boy in the school

And besides, Angeline is in that Mega-Popular category where she can probably go and work her wicked charms against boys like Chip, who is the number one cutest boy in the school.

So why does she always have to perform acts of **Beauty** around Hudson?

(Chip, like Madonna and Cher and Moses, only goes by his first name. I'm not sure anybody knows what his last name is.)

other one-Namers

PINK

TARZAN

BEEPY

THE SCIENCE OF BOY-OLOGY
Local Specimens

CHIP

CUTENESS RANKING: **1**

NON-MEAN AND HANDSOME ENOUGH TO BE IN A SHAVING CREAM COMMERCIAL

HUDSON RIVERS

CUTENESS RANKING: **8**

EASILY TRICKED INTO THINKING ANGELINE IS PRETTY. OTHERWISE EXCELLENT

ROSCO (CHIP'S DOG)

CUTENESS RANKING: **19**

STRICTLY SPEAKING NOT A BOY, BUT CUTER AND WAY MORE POPULAR THAN MOST TRUE BOYS

MIKE PINSETTI

CUTENESS RANKING: **ALMOST LAST**

MEAN AND MOUTHY. IF YOU MEET HIM TELL HIM ALL ABOUT SOAP.

THAT ONE KID

CUTENESS RANKING: **LAST**

DOES HE EVEN HAVE A NAME? WHO KNOWS. HE DOESN'T SEEM TO NEED ONE

Tuesday 03

Dear Dumb Diary,

Isabella came by after school to root through my magazines for those little paper perfume samples. She's got a top secret fragrance project she's working on. It's connected to her ongoing obsession with **Popularity,** I'm sure of it. Isabella is kind of an expert on Popularity, or so she says. (I know: Isabella belongs in a cage. But she is my best friend, **So One Does What One Must.**)

I looked everywhere before I finally found my magazines. Get this: they were in my parents' room. Hmmm! Looked like Mom had been flipping through them. I wonder if she's planning to do some sort of makeover on herself.

AN EXCELLENT MOM MAKEOVER

I heard about this girl whose mom had a makeover done on herself, and it was so good that afterward the mom looked younger and hotter than the daughter, which made her feel so guilty that she decided to have the makeover unmade. But when the cosmetologists tried to undo what had been done, they said that her body had absorbed the makeover, and now she was permanently afflicted with **Hotness.**

So her daughter came down with a form of **Embarrassment** that has to be treated by doctors.

I've never seen anything like it, nurse. This girl's mom actually embarrassed her daughter's butt off.

Honestly, I'm not terribly worried about Mom having a makeover. She can hardly makeover a bed.

mom makes a bed

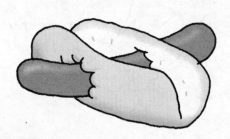

mom makes a hot dog

Wednesday 04

Dear Dumb Diary,

Here are what some people think are the worst things about my school:

When the Bus Drivers dress up for Halloween

When the teachers try talking cool

The unmistakable tangy flavor of horse organs in the cafeteria meatloaf.

But they're wrong...

The worst thing about school is my science class. I like the *idea* of science. I mean, it comforts me to know that Angeline's guts are no more glorious or appealing than the stuff you'd scoop out of a porcupine.

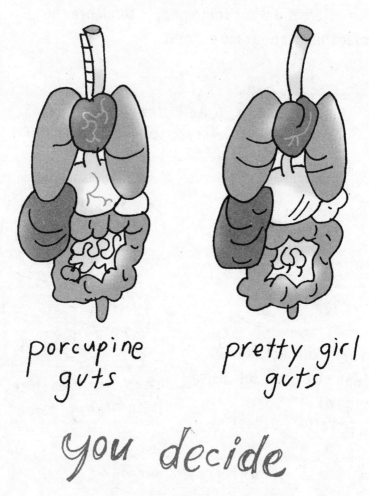

porcupine
guts

pretty girl
guts

you decide

But it's the whole chemistry part of it that I hate, like "this-kind-of-stuff-can-burn-through-this-junk," and "when-you-mix-this-with-that-then-whatever-will-explode." Science just doesn't seem to have much to do with what I'm trying to accomplish in my life right now, which is mainly the avoidance of science.

Are they even sure they want me in science class?

BOOM

At least Hudson Rivers is in my class. Isabella and I sometimes exchange scientific observations on Hudson.

Specimen chews gum at a rate of 32 chomps per minute

Specimen's right eye is 8% cuter than left eye

Specimen becomes mildly creeped out when it notices somebody counting its gum chews

Thursday 05

Dear Dumb Diary,

Tonight at dinner I realized that I am, once again, the youngest person in my family. My beagle, Stinker, was once younger than me, but by employing the totally unfair dog trick of aging seven years in just twelve months, Stinker went from peeing on the carpet to being old enough to drive in just a couple years. He is the only member of my family who has ever accomplished such an amazing feat, except I think I have an uncle who might have done it, too.

It is for this reason that I decided not to give Stinker my table scraps after dinner this evening. (Not because my uncle peed, but because Stinker made me the baby of the family *again*.)

Beagle actually trying to age 7 times faster than me.

15

This really made Stinker mad. Tonight, dinner was Chinese food — almost a beagle's favorite meal. (I wonder what they call Chinese food in China. They probably just say, "Here. Here's some of that food we always have.")

Friday 06

Dear Dumb Diary,

The vengeful beagle strikes again. To get back at me for not giving him my table scraps, Stinker ate a huge hole out of the backside of my only clean pair of jeans. (The second-best pair in the collection.) I know he would say he had to do it because he was so hungry from not having his normal gut-full of table scraps, but I know that he did it out of revenge.

How can I be so sure Stinker made the hole? It was in the most embarrassing place possible and it was **PERFECTLY** round. It looked like a tailor had chewed it.

Tailors are clothing experts and could probably bite a hole of any shape

So, I had to go with a pair of khaki pants that really had no business being out on a Friday. They're a Sunday pair of khakis. Sure, they started as a Friday pair of pants, but as cooler pants were purchased, the khakis were demoted.

I paired them with a shirt that was a *serious* Friday shirt, hoping to boost the khakis' confidence and give them the feeling that maybe they were somehow becoming more fashionable. It totally worked, of course, as pants are really stupid. You would think that a pair of khakis would notice that, currently, the most popular pants at my school are jeans, faded to just the right shade of blue.

PHASES IN THE LIFE OF PANTS

PHASE 1
Brand new and in style. Happiest time in a pant's life. Wear at any time.

PHASE 2
Slightly out of style or with taco stain. Wear on Sundays only.

PHASE 3
Hole bitten out of fanny by dog or tailor. Wear only as part of Hobo Costume.

Of course, I don't *have* any jeans that are the perfect shade of blue. If I awoke one morning to discover that I had a pair that WAS the right shade of blue, I would just assume that they weren't my pants, it wasn't my house, and it wasn't me who had just woken up.

Other signals that could have indicated I was in the wrong house...

Dad encourages massive make-up abuse

Dog is not mean and spends several minutes a day not licking itself

Mom prepares a nonstinking casserole which family voluntarily eats

Saturday 07

Dear Dumb Diary,

The most incredible thing happened today. Isabella and I saw Angeline, but not at school. It's always so weird when you know somebody only from school, but then you see them in the real world. It's like when you walk in on a clown, and he's only wearing his underpants. (Long story: Bad birthday party experience. Don't like clowns anymore.)

Anyway, Angeline was in the park, and she was playing with these two little kids who Isabella and I figured were her little sisters. But the little sisters did not have Angeline's great looks (**Nobody cares anyway, Angeline!**), thereby verifying what we have always just suspected about Angeline: **SHE'S BEEN PLASTIC-SURGEONED.** Probably nothing on her is an original part.

It would cost a fortune to do that much plastic surgery on somebody who started out as ugly as we hope Angeline did, so we figure that Angeline's dad is some big doctor.

On top of everything else, she's probably RICH.

ANALYSIS of THE Surgery they probably did on ANGELINE

HORN REMOVAL $1500

HAIR DYED AND MADE PERMANENTLY GOOD SMELLING $1800

CONTACT LENSES $800

NOSE JOB $4200

WING TRIM $2000

FANGECTOMY $1800

TAIL CUT OFF

EXTREME MANICURE $47

KNEES DE-KNOBBED

FEET PROBABLY LEFT THE SAME

Just when I thought I knew everything there was about Angeline that bugged me, it turns out she's also loaded.

Angeline taking a BATH IN PURE MONEY

Jewel encrusted soap

HOT AND COLD RUNNING DIAMONDS

RUG OF EXTRAORDINARY FLUFFINESS

Sunday 08

Dear Dumb Diary,

It's Sunday. Also known as **Homework Day**. Every weekend I tell myself that I'm going to finish my homework when I get home on Friday afternoon, and then I tell myself I'm going to do it Saturday morning, and then I tell myself I'll do it Saturday night, and then I tell myself to get off my back, and why am I always nagging myself, and then I call myself a name and have to apologize to myself.

And then I have to do all my homework on Sunday.

Tomorrow is school and I can't risk another wardrobe-munching by Stinker, so I gave him table scraps from dinner.

How Beagles enjoy their scraps

Sniff suspiciously for eleven minutes

SNIFF
SNURF
SNURF
SNIFF

cautiously pick up with front teeth

PINCE

Hork it down in one gulp and choke to death a little

GWARF
ACK
GAG
GULP

Monday 09

Dear Dumb Diary,

Okay. Who wants to buy a beagle cheap? Remember the other night we had Chinese food? Stinker didn't get any scraps and that's why he ate my pants.

Last night I gave him scraps, but Mom had cooked some sort of **Goo Casserole** and it had somehow slipped my mind that few living things except bacteria enjoy my mom's cooking. (Mom is a good mom and everything, but she's not very good at traditional mom things, like cooking and cleaning and washing clothes.) So *guess* what Stinker did?

pure love and joy

utter disgust

It looks like Stinker quietly crept through the house, carefully sorted through the laundry Mom had just done, found the absolute **best**-looking pair of jeans I own, and ate an even bigger hole. Through the front this time!

↑
pure
evil

Does anybody **know** why dogs do the things they do? I think they might do some of them (like *you-know-what*) just to see if they can get their picture in the newspaper for being the **GROSSEST DOG ON EARTH.** But why Stinker is gnawing through my pants is anybody's guess.

The Daily News

DOG DOES GROSSEST THING ANYBODY EVER HEARD OF

"SO DID WE" CLAIM OTHER LOCAL DOGS

The couch it happened behind

I could propose the question in science class, except it would draw attention to my pants and I had to wear khakis again today.

Our science class works like this: Everybody has a lab partner. A lab partner is a person that you do all the experiments with while you both wish the other one was Sally Winthorpe, who is this really smart girl who probably has a brain for every single organ in her body, because she's sort of tiny and her head is just not big enough to fit that much smartness in. Although I'm not sure what being that smart can get you.

Sally was Isabella's partner for a long time, but then they got switched. Of course now she's Angeline's partner, so I'm sure Angeline never has to do any work. Which, added to the whole being loaded thing, really kind of bites.

Isabella talked too much and Palmer switched them

For now my lab partner is Isabella — whose head is plenty big — but there's a chance she's using part of it for a lunch box or laundry hamper. She has been conducting this top secret science experiment involving collecting every single one of those perfume sample cards that they put in magazines, and combining them into one massive **SUPERFRAGRANCE** that she says will smell as good as every known good smell in the Universe, combined. She has been doing this in science class because she already has about seventy of them crammed in an old baby food jar she's kept hidden in a cabinet in the science room. Just taking the lid off the thing to stuff another one in requires her to wear the science class safety glasses.

Isabella has been having a sinus problem, so she can hardly smell at all. But without the glasses, she says the vapor could still blind her for life.

Angeline and her genius partner, Sally, spotted us doing a perfume deposit today. Angeline, though beautiful and therefore fundamentally evil, didn't tattle. Call her **conceited**. Call her **stuck-up**. Call her **self-centered**. I mean it. Somebody go get the phone and call her.

But the truth is that she could have squealed but didn't. My theory is that at Angeline's lofty level of **MEGA-POPULARITY,** a snitcher is frowned upon. (At one point I thought I might have even seen her smile a little, but I've seen crocodiles do the same thing, so I can't be sure what it means.)

QUIZ
Which one is the cold-blooded reptile and which one is the crocodile?

Tuesday 10

Dear Dumb Diary,

Isabella's sinus problem is still bugging her. She can't smell **anything**. She says her sinuses are bad enough that she could park in handicapped spaces if she were old enough to drive. Since she isn't, she says that the law allows her to just stand in them.

Wednesday 11

Dear Dumb Diary,

    Isabella needed to make another perfume deposit today. I stood in front of her so that Mrs. Palmer, the science teacher, couldn't see what we were doing. (Mrs. Palmer replaced our previous teacher, Mr. Tweeds, who fell and broke his hip, which is what all old people do sooner or later because their skeletons are as brittle and cracky as pretzel rods. He's like 48 or something.) But it turns out that Mrs. Palmer, like most adults, doesn't really care **exactly** what you're doing when you are doing something that you're trying to hide. (Adults are like frogs that snap bugs out of the air without first getting a good look at them: Could be a butterfly. Could be a killer bee.) So Mrs. Palmer just separated us as lab partners.

Mrs. Palmer believes that switching partners whenever there is a problem is a good idea. Until today, I never believed her.

Mrs. Palmer is a teacher so naturally I assumed she would never do anything good for me. But...

You know how I said that adults are like frogs? Here's another aspect of their froggishness: Frogs are sometimes princes deep down inside. Or princesses, in Mrs. Palmer's case. (Although this particular princess would need a queen-size throne for **Her Royal Hineyness**.)

Mrs. Palmer had to split up another set of lab partners in order to separate Isabella and me. Sure, she *could* have paired me up with Margaret Parker, total reject. But she didn't. Dear, sweet Mrs. Palmer presented to me, like a humongous plate of cookies, my new lab partner, **HUDSON RIVERS**. She gave Hudson's old partner, Margaret Parker, to Isabella, like a plate of wet socks.

Don't get me wrong, Dumb Diary, Margaret is okay, I guess. She's kind of nice, but she's a **pencil chewer,** and most non-beavers find that a bit repulsive. (Isabella says that Margaret is a "GERD," which is a **GIRL NERD.**)

Isabella's Terms for Girls

GERD
(GIRL NERD)

MORONICA
(FEMALE IDIOT)

CHOCK
(chick jock)

COW
(WOMAN BULL)

Isabella used the opportunity to share with me *(again)* more about her theories on Popularity. She says that Unpopularity is contagious, and you can catch it the same way you catch the **Flu** or **Bad Dancing.** Honestly, though, I don't believe that Unpopularity is a real Force of Nature, like Gravity or Deliciousness. I told her that she should be more open-minded about her new partner. And that deep down inside, Margaret is probably a good person.

Then I realized what a beautiful and sensitive thing I had said, and I imagined that maybe one day I might open a big sanctuary where all the **Social Rejects** could live and run free and never have to worry about wedgies again. Plus, I could sell tickets to people to come and look at them.

Little Billy feeds one of my captive rejects its favorite snack

Thursday 12, 3:45 AM

Dear Dumb Diary,

I can't believe I stayed up this late. It's like, the middle of the night. There was this scary movie on TV tonight about this little girl who finds this old doll that's haunted, which anybody could tell was going to be haunted because she was a really sweet girl, and she really loved the doll, and there is just no way a movie is going to let a sweet little girl be happy with her doll. Not if it's a good movie, anyway.

But now I am in serious trouble because I still have science homework to finish and I blame my mom who is the one who let me have this TV in my room after I begged two years nonstop for it. (I mean, a kid can't spoil herself, Dumb Diary, am I right? My spoilage is Mom's fault.)

I'd like to write more, but I'm really tired and I have to get this homework finished.

If I don't, Mrs. Palmer is going to bite my

Friday 13

Dear Dumb Diary,

    That's right. I fell asleep last night without finishing my science homework. Which means, as predicted, that Mrs. Palmer bit my head off. And then it got worse. Figuring that the problem was with the new lab partner arrangement, she switched Hudson with Margaret. Now Margaret is my lab partner, and Isabella has Hudson.

Symptoms of Hudson Withdrawal
(exhibited ONLY in private)

And since I missed the homework, Mrs. Palmer suggested that Margaret and I get together over the weekend to get me caught up. And Margaret said, right there in front of many Popular ears, between munchy chomps on a damp pencil, "Great. What time should I come over, Jamie?"

If I had been less tired, and outfitted in more confident clothing (thanks, Stinker), I might have come up with a cool comeback. Maybe the coolest one ever, but now we'll never know because I sleepily said, "whenever," and Mike Pinsetti, who used to be in the business of making up nicknames for people, but is currently experimenting with other forms of annoying harassment, made a loud kissy-kissy sound. As most people know, in some parts of the world, the kissy-kissy sound of a bully is enough to actually legally marry two people to each other.

Kissy kissy
smoochy
smerchy
kissy

In this case, it suggested that perhaps Margaret and I were now best friends, and I could feel the Popularity flying off me like the delicate petals of a beautiful flower that somebody had stuck into the spinning blades of a fan.

Afterward, of course, Isabella didn't miss the opportunity to point out that I should be more open-minded about my new lab partner. I told her that open-minded is what you are if you get hit in the head with an ax, and I felt plenty open-minded enough.

Anyway, Dumb Diary, Margaret is coming over tomorrow.

Saturday 14

Dear Dumb Diary,

As foretold, Margaret came over. We finished the homework junk, and I realized that even though at first I had thought that Margaret was sort of an Unpopular Goof, after I got to know her a little, I realized that deep down, she was much worse than that.

often the inner person is way grosser

If there was anything to this Unpopularity infection thing, I was in serious trouble.

Fortunately, Isabella stopped by and we had a minute to talk privately while Margaret was in the bathroom, doing whatever it is that Unpopular people do in there. (Make themselves LESS presentable?)

The secret products of the UNPOPULAR

HAIR UNCONDITIONER

Pork-color contact lenses

STEW-SCENTED DEODORANT

Isabella had stopped by out of concern. She was concerned about her jar of SuperFragrance, which was gone, probably found by Mrs. Palmer. She was concerned that her lab partnership with Hudson didn't bother me enough. I assured her that it did, but since she was my best friend, I decided not to dwell on it. And she was most concerned that Margaret could drag down my Popularity, and since I'm friends with Isabella, it could affect her Popularity as well.

But Isabella had the solution. . . .

And it was an excellent one:
A MAKEOVER.

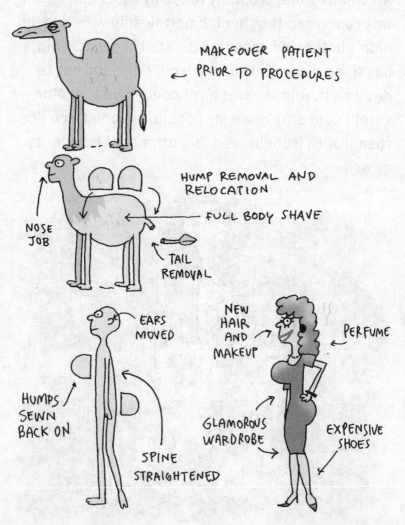

MAKEOVER PATIENT
← PRIOR TO PROCEDURES

HUMP REMOVAL AND
RELOCATION

FULL BODY SHAVE

NOSE
JOB

TAIL
REMOVAL

NEW
HAIR
AND
MAKEUP

PERFUME

EARS
MOVED

HUMPS
SEWN
BACK ON

GLAMOROUS
WARDROBE

EXPENSIVE
SHOES

SPINE
STRAIGHTENED

See? Makeovers totally work!

Just like on TV. We will help Margaret fix herself up a little, and thereby undo whatever damage she has done to us. Like all of our plans, this is surely a great idea.

Other great ideas of ours

the 9-foot-long french fry

some kind of pill you could take and be instantly healthy

the 18-foot-long french fry

I was trying to figure out a delicate way to suggest the makeover, but Isabella had already come up with a gentle way to introduce the idea to Margaret.

Margaret did not take this as hard as you might think. She seemed kind of sickly grateful for the attention. I felt a little bad and might have pulled out right there, except for how much fun it is to put makeup on somebody else's face. Tomorrow, Isabella and I, **Known Experts on Fashion,** will begin **PROJECT MARGARET.**

My Incredible Makeup Skills at Work

Frankenstein

The Mummy

Wolfman

Sunday 15

Dear Dumb Diary,

    Project Margaret begins.

    Amazingly, Mom was totally okay with taking us all to the mall today. I was fully prepared for a huge argument, followed by some crying, an apology, and finally, a trip to the mall. Mom's saying yes right away saved me about four minutes.

I had saved up a LOT, too.

On the way to the mall, we passed the park, and saw Angeline again. But this time the kids looked entirely different from before. Obviously, her plastic surgeon dad had already started cutting the kids up to make perfect little miniature Angelines out of them.

Angeline's sick joy

Here's How those kids looked Before

Here's How they look now

We took Margaret around to the best stores at the mall. It was a little bit spiritual, because Margaret had not even heard of a lot of them. Isabella and I felt a little bit like we were doing something profound and wonderful, like teaching a gorilla sign language.

Margaret started to chicken out a little at the clothes and accessories that Isabella and I had selected. She was craving some pencils pretty badly, but finally, she caved because we used **Peer Pressure** against her.

Bet I know what Margaret was thinking of

Adults think that Peer Pressure can influence what kids do, but it's actually a thousand times more powerful than that.

Obi-Wan Kenobi's Jedi mind tricks have nothing on Peer Pressure. Seriously. Isabella and I could have had Darth Vader in a miniskirt and braids in about five minutes.

We dropped Margaret off at Sally Winthorpe's house after the mall. I guess Sally had asked her over or something. (Maybe a Big Pencil Dinner.) But who cares? Because the main thing of the day or, as French people call it, *le main ting of ze day,* was **MY** new jeans! When we were at the mall, Mom found me a pair of **Bellazure Jeans.** They are the coolest jeans ever made and she bought them for me without my even having to ask. **Why did Mom buy me these really cool and really expensive pants??** I may never know.

But who cares?

The utter rapture of brand-new jeans

Yeah, yeah. Mission accomplished with Margaret. She'll probably be a little bit better off. But now *I* own the coolest pair of jeans ever.

Stinker, I hope you are reading this, because I want you to know that an enraged girl can pick up a beagle by his fat little tail and hurl him directly into the core of the Sun if she is sufficiently antagonized, pants-wise.

So long, Munchy

Monday 16

Dear Dumb Diary,

    I wore my new jeans to school today, and I felt like I was the most beautiful bottom-half-of-a-girl on Earth. I was just getting ready to drink up all the compliments when Margaret walked into science class.

Aren't I adorable?

Then I heard something that I had never heard before. It's not a sound you often hear. It was sort of a soft, wet, popping sound. I realize now that it was the sound of twenty-six jaws dropping open at exactly the same time.

Margaret was, well, she was **GORGEOUS.** Her hair, her perfume, her jewelry, her new clothes, were working together like a symphony orchestra comprised of the rare supermodels who are smart enough to read music.

Margaret

Isabella and I took a little bit of pride in it, feeling sort of like the people who own those incredible dogs at dog shows. You know what I mean: We're not the dog, but without us the dog would be licking a fire hydrant somewhere instead of looking like a million bucks. (That's SEVEN million bucks in dog money.)

Note: Nobody is currently prepared to accuse Margaret of this sort of fire hydrant lickage.

Margaret was so happy. And Isabella was happy. And I was happy. And Hudson was happy. *(grrr!)*

And okay, I wasn't. There was something vaguely sinister in the air, and I'm not sure what it was.

Tuesday 17

Dear Dumb Diary,

Here's a peculiar scientific phenomenon I learned in class today and, like all of the important scientific discoveries, it involves choosing your deodorant wisely.

For instance, these choices not so good

Margaret borrowed my pencil today. She must have forgotten that she was no longer a Gerd, because when I looked up she had it in her mouth and was enjoying what could only be described as a *relationship* with it. It was one of those moments when you find yourself looking around for something to hit somebody with. (I have this moment about fifteen times a day.)

But then this soothing breeze of fragrant excellence comes wafting off Margaret and I felt, like, soothed. That is one excellent deodorant. I even let her keep eating my pencil.

But the soothery didn't last forever. Is soothery a word? Whatever. By lunch I was no longer soothed. And Isabella was visibly shaken.

Sure, she's always visibly shaken, but today, she was picking up a really strange vibe. Bad Mojo. Evil Juju.

Isabella, who is sharply attuned to this sort of thing, walked in and instantly observed that the precarious **Lunch Table Dynamic** had been upset.

She said that some of the Medium-Popular kids were sitting with the Less-Than-Medium-Popular kids. For a moment I thought she was nuts, until I saw Margaret was sitting at **THE ULTRA-MEGA-POPULAR** table. Isabella said this really should not happen. For Margaret to escalate that quickly, it could destroy the Natural Order of the Universe, and worse. . . .

ISABELLA FREAKS

Isabella said that it meant that we had fallen a notch. By accidentally inserting Margaret in at such a high level of popularity, we had actually pushed everybody below her down. She said we're suddenly tumbling into the Pit of Zero Popularity. Can she be right? Is there really such a thing as Popularity, or is it all some sort of weird scientific theory?

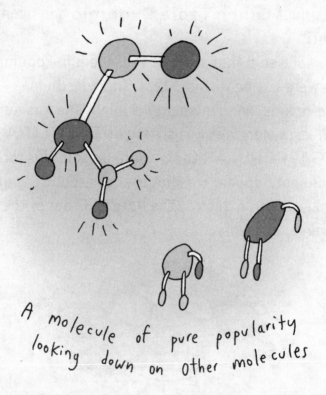

A molecule of pure popularity looking down on other molecules

Wednesday 18

Dear Dumb Diary,

Wore the New Pants again. I didn't wear them yesterday, of course. You can't wear them **every** day, or people will say you only have one cool pair of pants, which they would be jerks for being right about.

Thankfully, Stinker had not gone mental on them, but I don't know if that's because we are friends again, or because I've been hanging them in my closet where stubby little beagle legs can't reach.

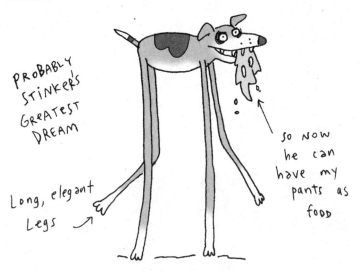

PROBABLY STINKER'S GREATEST DREAM

Long, elegant Legs

SO NOW he can have my pants as food

Isabella and I may have destroyed **The Entire Universe.** (I, for one, do not believe the Universe should be this fragile, because it's where I keep all my stuff.)

But here's what makes me think we destroyed it. Today at lunch, somebody was missing at the Mega-Popular table. Isabella was right. We did such a magnificent job on Margaret's makeover that she has bumped everybody. She has even bumped . . . Angeline!

It was a truly beautiful moment. **Angeline had been taken down a notch!** It was the most beautiful lunchtime moment since the time Miss Bruntford, the cafeteria monitor, slipped on a smear of creamed corn and gave an involuntary figure skating performance that ended with a double axel into a face-plant.

I love figure skating

But, just like *that* beautiful moment —
which was shattered by our having to stare at
Miss Bruntford's massive underpants until the
paramedics arrived (You're not allowed to move
somebody in that condition. We also learned
that tossing Tater Tots at her wasn't a good idea,
either.) — *this* beautiful moment was shattered by
the realization that if Angeline had been demoted,
then we were even lower than we thought.

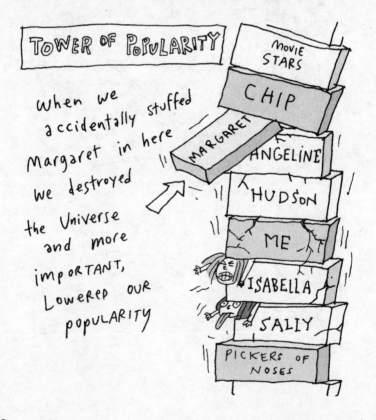

TOWER OF POPULARITY

MOVIE STARS

CHIP

MARGARET

ANGELINE

HUDSON

ME

ISABELLA

SALLY

PICKERS OF NOSES

When we
accidentally stuffed
Margaret in here
we destroyed
the Universe
and more
importANT,
Lowered our
popularity

And Angeline was, in her typical deceptive way, not acting like it bothered her.

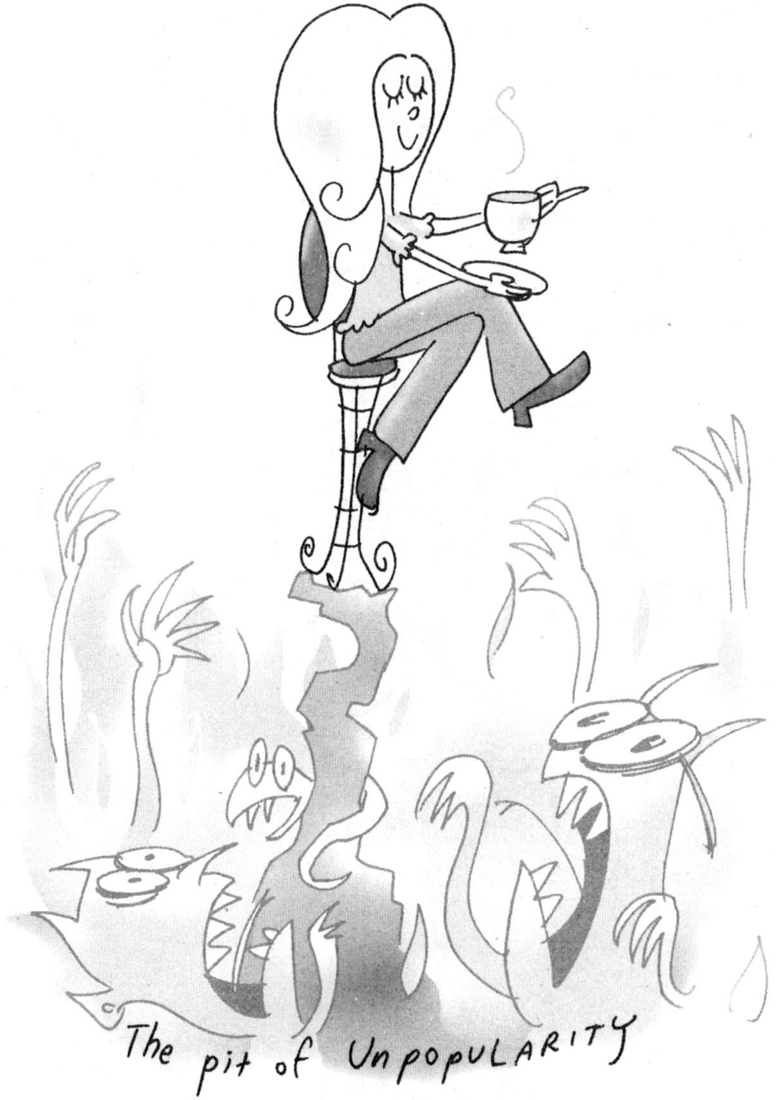
The pit of UnpopuLARITY

As we were standing there alternately blaming each other for making over Margaret in the first place, we noticed Hudson walking over to the Mid-Popular table and, just as he did, my pants — How can I put this? — decided to *join the conversation.* You get my drift, Dumb Diary? My pants cut the cheese. Let one fly. Baked a batch of brownies. Got the picture?

I know what you're thinking, Dumb Diary, pants can't get gas. And yet . . .

Fortunately for me, Isabella, who comes from a large family and is therefore an expert on swiftly blaming others, pretended to be horrified by some confused innocent kid nearby. She made Hudson think that the noise came from **Confused Innocent Kid,** or **Stinkypants,** as I have learned since lunch that he has come to be called. By everyone.

Of course, I admire Isabella for being so good at getting others in trouble, but she didn't believe me when I told her that it was the pants all by themselves, and not me.

STINKY PANTS

ISABELLA'S Big family has taught her how to efficiently ruin the lives of others swiftly

Families are the Best!

There's no **WAY** Isabella would have believed that the pants actually made me walk past the Mega-Popular Table, and that they also made me bump the table a little bit as if I was some sort of angry tough kid looking for trouble. Although now that I think about it, there's that one kid who actually bumps into *everything,* including lunch tables, and he's never looking for anything except his hat, which is routinely hidden from him.

What is with these pants, anyway?

Can PANTS make people think you are a huge DERF, like BUMP-into-everything KID?

Thursday 19

Dear Dumb Diary,

So tell me, Dumb Diary, if you were something small and ghastly, like a tiny, hairy creature that lived in a shower drain, and two beautiful fairy princesses took the time out from their very busy schedules to transform you into some sort of flying sparkling unicorn with diamond hooves that could shoot rainbow butterflies out its ears, would you just decide to throw it all away and cram yourself back into the shower drain?

HORRIBLE thing Re-crams itself

Well, that is exactly what Margaret did. She showed up today in science class without the new clothes, without the new jewelry, without the makeup.

ugly old hair

ugly old HAIR Accessory

ugly old clothes

ugly old beaver impersonation

ugly old shoe

ugly old other shoe

Isabella and I were floored. This meant that everything was back to normal. I accidentally let out this big cheer, and Mrs. Palmer dropped an alcohol burner, and then the whole room smelled like that substitute teacher who got fired last month for falling asleep in class.

Other Famous Substitute Teachers

— Mr. Stupid McClueless

The Sugar Substitute

The Tuna Sub

Of course, Mrs. Palmer employed her strategy of switching lab partners around. This means that now my lab partner is Mike Pinsetti, and Margaret is partnered up with some other kid, I forget who.

But I was so happy about Margaret's terrible judgment that this new partnerfication didn't really sink in.

In fact, as we switched seats, I even smiled at Mike Pinsetti, which made him try to smile back (*I think*), but it looked more like he had his hand caught in a car door. I may be the first person who has ever smiled directly at Mike's face.

Yes, indeed, everything seemed pretty wonderful until lunch. That's when we saw IT.

STRAIN
THROB

PINSETTI TRIES TO PERFORM SMILING

Margaret was sitting at the Mega-Popular table, talking to Chip, in her old, pencil-eating-shower-drain-creature form. Even Sally Winthorpe seemed to take notice. It was as though the very **Wonderbread of Reality** had been besmeared by the Peanut Butter of Illusion, and further obscured by the Grape Jelly of — oh, I don't know, I'm trying to make it all relate to lunch.

The simple fact is that, according to Isabella, we're much, much lower on the Popularity scale now than ever before, since it appears that Margaret has ascended on her own *(yuck)* merits.

Friday 20

Dear Dumb Diary,

Isabella came over tonight. She had some movie she had rented. (It was called *Terror at Your Throat*.) We started watching it, and it was about a haunted necklace and how bad things happened to this family after they got it. During the movie, Isabella jumped up and screamed that the necklace was exactly like my pants, which made Stinker commit Urine. It was probably because he is not used to people screaming while he is fast asleep. Still, I had to spank him a little for it.

Anyway, Isabella said it wasn't the makeover that boosted Margaret's Popularity and forced us down. It was the pants. She said it wasn't my loud "yahoo" in science that got me switched again so that I'm science partners with Known Goon, Mike Pinsetti. It was the pants. And she said it wasn't me who had done **you-know-what** all over Hudson Rivers. **IT WAS THE PANTS.**

SUPERNATURAL
EVIL

PLUS
GAS

I pointed out that I hadn't exactly gassed all over him. A debate followed, but she was firm on this point: The pants were to blame. **THE PANTS ARE HAUNTED.**

WATCH 20-MINUTE COMMERCIAL ABOUT A CHICKEN ROASTER

TASTE KIWI SHAMPOO TO SEE if it's as good as it smells

CALL HUDSON AND HANG UP. THIRTY TIMES.

PANTS MADE ME DO

IMAGINE TRAGIC EVENT IN WHICH everybody I know dies and I have to carry on prettily.

STROKE Roof of mouth with toothbrush and cause four-hour tickle.

Right now, Isabella is calling her mom to get permission to sleep over. I don't think I want to be in my room alone with the pants all night, and we plan to drive the spirits away tomorrow.

Saturday 21

Dear Dumb Diary,

Isabella's first idea was to tear the pants to shreds. But I wanted to see if we could just drive the wicked spirits out of them without the rippage. I mean, c'mon. They *were* pretty cool pants after all.

Isabella's next idea was to use a Ouija board to contact the tormented ghosts in my pants, but I don't have a Ouija board, so we tried to do it with a Monopoly game. Sadly, we didn't really make much progress, except we decided to try to make charm bracelets with the dog and race car pieces.

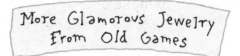

More Glamorous Jewelry From Old Games

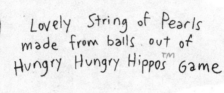

Lovely String of Pearls made from balls out of Hungry Hungry Hippos™ Game

Spooky Voodoo Necklace made from old Operation™ Game Bones

Pierced earrings made from Mr. Potato Head's™ Ears

I thought we should light candles and speak some sort of mystic chant. We're not really well-informed on chants, so we said the Pledge of Allegiance, which, though technically speaking is not a mystic chant, still sounds pretty creepy when you say it low and zombie-like in a dark room with flashlights. (Dad doesn't allow lit candles in my room, so we had to make do.)

Freaked ourselves out a little

Finally, we decided to just pound the evil out of the pants, and this took the form of laying the pants out in the backyard and stomping all over them in various evil-destroying karate-like moves. It occurred to us both at the exact same time just how dumb we looked, so we took them inside and stuffed them into the washing machine. They were torn up pretty good. Maybe all it will take now is a little sudsing.

The point when we thought we might not be banishing evil and we might be huge spazzes.

Sunday 22

Dear Dumb Diary,

We walked to Isabella's house this morning, and when we passed the park we saw Angeline again. It looked like her dad had Plastic-Surgeoned those little kids back to their original appearances. Why would somebody do that? You can't just scribble out a plastic surgery and start over.

Or can you?

Late-breaking Thoughts

Could there be another, simpler explanation? I asked Isabella, and she said no. She said that the most obvious answer was that Angeline's plastic-surgeon father was doing and undoing operations on her younger sisters in order to make them look like different kids on alternating weekends. Also, it appeared that he had some sort of way to change their heights.

START   CHANGED   CHANGED BACK   CHANGED AGAIN

You have to hand it to Isabella. When she's right, she's right.

When I got home, I peeked in the washing machine and the pants were gone. Hmm . . . **Demon Pants** mysteriously vanished. The only reasonable thing to do was to run screaming upstairs to my room.

Other times when screaming is necessary...

Monster is chasing you and your high heels are too cute to abandon

Eaten by Ants

Gramps accidentally shoots a moon

Monday 23

Dear Dumb Diary,

    THE PANTS ARE BACK. This morning when I woke up, there they were, hanging on a hanger, looking brand-new, and totally haunted. They had mysteriously healed themselves. Also, I think they were staring at me.

    I moved slowly and carefully around the jeans and reached into my drawer for another pair, only to discover that Stinker had chewed one of his big round holes in my last pair of non-evil jeans.

No jeans left! I was so angry that I dropped everything and made a big sign. It says, "Have You Been Mean to Your Beagle Today?" in glitter. **GLITTER,** Stinker. That means I *really, really* mean it. People use glitter on signs only when they are dead serious. And I put it up on my wall where he could see it all the time.

GRIND
SMASH
CRAM
MASH

HAVE YOU
BEEN
MEAN
YOUR
BEAGLE
TODAY?

Before I left for school, I cut up four hot dogs (possibly Stinker's favorite food) and put them in Stinker's dish. Then after he got a good look at them, I threw them out in the yard so that Stinker could sit by the window all day and watch the neighbor's cats sit out there and eat his hot dogs.

Tuesday 24

Dear Dumb Diary,

     Margaret continues to travel in the Mega-Popular circle in spite of her undeniable Gerdness (or would it be Gerditude?). The Evil of the Pants is strong. Indeed, they are twisting the very fiber of our Universe. Up is down, left is right, over there is over there now (I'm pointing).

Haunted By the Demon Denim

Isabella says our only hope is plastic surgery. She says that if we can get Angeline's dad to do some work on us, we might be able to claw our way back out of the Unpopularity pit.

pit. clawing is just murder on the nails →

I suppose it only makes good sense that you can feel better about yourself by letting somebody cut up your face, but I'm not sure exactly how that works. Isabella assured me that if we don't like what Angeline's dad does, he can always change us back like he does on Angeline's ever-changing little sisters. I guess I should consider it.

I told Isabella to ask Sally Winthorpe what she thinks, since she had offered to help Isabella and Margaret with their science homework after school.

Isabella says that Plastic surgery makes you Beautiful

I just noticed my "Be Mean to Your Beagle" sign again.

I took Stinker into the bathroom and weighed him on the scale and told him that he was twenty pounds overweight.

I really don't want to be mean to Stinker anymore, but he has to learn his lesson.

Wednesday 25

Dear Dumb Diary,

    The pants are stronger than we thought. Even wadded up in the bottom of my closet, they still exert a destructive force at school, and here's how:
    Margaret and Isabella's science homework was **WRONG.** Sally is never wrong. The only explanation is evil, jinxed jeans. Mrs. Palmer, like always, did a partner switch, and this time she put Sally and Hudson together, which seemed to make Sally sort of happy. (If I didn't know better, I would swear she was crushing on him a little. Do smart girls do that? I have no idea.)

Can a smart girl have a crush?

OR WOULD SHE HAVE A BRAIN WHERE HER HEART SHOULD BE?

After school, Isabella made me help her corner Angeline. You are not going to believe how **WEIRD** this turned out to be, Dumb Diary.

Isabella is pretty blunt, so she just comes out and asks Angeline if her rich doctor dad will do plastic surgery on us.

Angeline looked pretty puzzled. She said that her dad worked in an office. He's an accountant.

I asked what about the little sisters we see her with in the park. Her dad keeps doing plastic surgery on them.

Those aren't her sisters. Those are kids she babysits. And they don't keep changing. They're different kids.

I know what you're thinking, Dumb Diary: Why does a rich girl need to babysit?

It turns out that Angeline is **NOT RICH.** She babysits because she needs to. She's saving up to buy — get this — a pair of Bellazure Jeans.

Angeline wants me to believe the lies I keep telling about her

But none of that is the weird part. Here's the weird part: Angeline and I wear the exact same size jeans. How can that be? She looks like a Greek statue, and I look like the place where somebody started to carve a girl and then gave up halfway through the project.

we wear the same size? I didn't know we were even the same species.

Isabella offered to sell Angeline my jeans at half price and Angeline said okay. (Not a big surprise, really, that Isabella would make that move. Once, Isabella tried to sell somebody my shoes, and I was wearing them at the time.)

I started to tell Angeline that they were possessed by some sort of horrible otherworldly force, and Isabella gave me an elbow in the ribs. I just had to tell Angeline after finding out she was my **size-sister.**

She didn't care. She said she didn't believe in otherworldly forces. It's your funeral, Angeline.

Otherwordly Garment Spookiness

HAUNTED PANTS
(I CAN PROVE THESE)

POSSESSED UNDERWEAR
(THESE SEEM LIKELY)

VOODOO MUUMUU,
(I HOPE THESE
EXIST. IT'S A
GOOD RHYME)

Thursday 26

Dear Dumb Diary,

What a day. What a day.

Mom came in and woke me up for school and noticed my anti-beagle sign. I explained to her what Stinker had been doing to my jeans, but that I was getting tired of being mean to him, anyway, and would probably take it down soon. I was thinking of replacing it with a gentler sign saying, "Be Mean to Your Beagle When He Deserves It." Also, I was planning to diminish the imposing threat of the message through the use of less glitter.

Mom may have noticed where a Beagle's Face was mushed into the sign

Then Mom dropped her bomb. Stinker had **NOT** made those holes.

After our little discussion about clothing a few weeks ago, Mom had decided to try to "get with it." She found out that the lighter-blue denim was the cool jean of the moment, and she looked through my magazines for tips on bleaching jeans. She couldn't find any, so she decided to just give it a whirl on her own.

I love my mom

But she's...

you know...

ALL

MOMMISH

She had spilled some bleach on my jeans the first time, and it turns out that bleach can eat a big round hole right through a pair of pants. She tried a couple more times, but those were not any better, you'll remember. She felt so bad she bought me the Bellazure Jeans.

Ah, **GUILT.** And some people say it's a bad thing.

Later, my mom found the Bellazure Jeans that Isabella and I had destroyed in the washing machine on Sunday. Not knowing that Isabella and I had attempted to stomp the Evil out of them, Mom assumed that SHE was responsible for wrecking them in the wash. She rushed to the mall and bought a brand-new pair, which she hung on a hanger in my room. (So they *didn't* mysteriously heal themselves.)

I looked over at Stinker, who was listening to all of this with what could only be described as a scowl, even though I'm not sure a dog *can* scowl with lips that are pretty much just flaps.

I wonder if dogs can hold a grudge.

Isabella's sinus problem cleared up. Why is that worth mentioning? The day got weirder. You'll see, Dumb Diary.

ISABELLA'S NOSE fiNALLY DOES Something

In science class today, I noticed that Margaret seemed a little more, I don't know, Gerd-like.

I also noticed that Hudson and Sally Winthorpe, the brand-new lab partners, were really chatting it up. I mean, **BIG-TIME.** They were laughing and smiling, and it was like they were the only two people in the room.

HUDSON

SALLY

The evil of the pants is indeed powerful

Then Sally flashed a quick glance my way, and I saw something in her eyes: **GUILT.** I recognized it as exactly the same precise expression that Stinker had not had about the pants, but Mom had.

When Isabella passed by Sally, she stopped for a second, and I could tell she was confused by something. And it was more than Isabella's normal confused look.

Other normal confused looks

Science class was the same as ever: chemicals this and chemicals that. When the bell rang, I went out into the hall, and Angeline strolled up to me. She wanted the pants, and I pulled them out of my backpack and handed them to her. She dashed to the bathroom to try them on.

From inside the science room, I heard Isabella and Sally Winthorpe squawking about something. Then I heard a jar break, and the fire alarm went off.

Everybody in the whole school filed outside, and Isabella dragged Sally over to talk to me.

Isabella is probably tough enough to be a girl bully (A GULLY)

Isabella said, "I was right. Tell her, Sally."

And Sally Winthorpe, smartest girl in my grade (maybe the school) explained:

Sally had taken an interest in Isabella's **Top Secret SuperFragrance** project. She was the one who had taken Isabella's jarful of concentrated perfume samples. And she had done it for . . .

SALLY

DRAMATIZATION OF CRIME SCENE

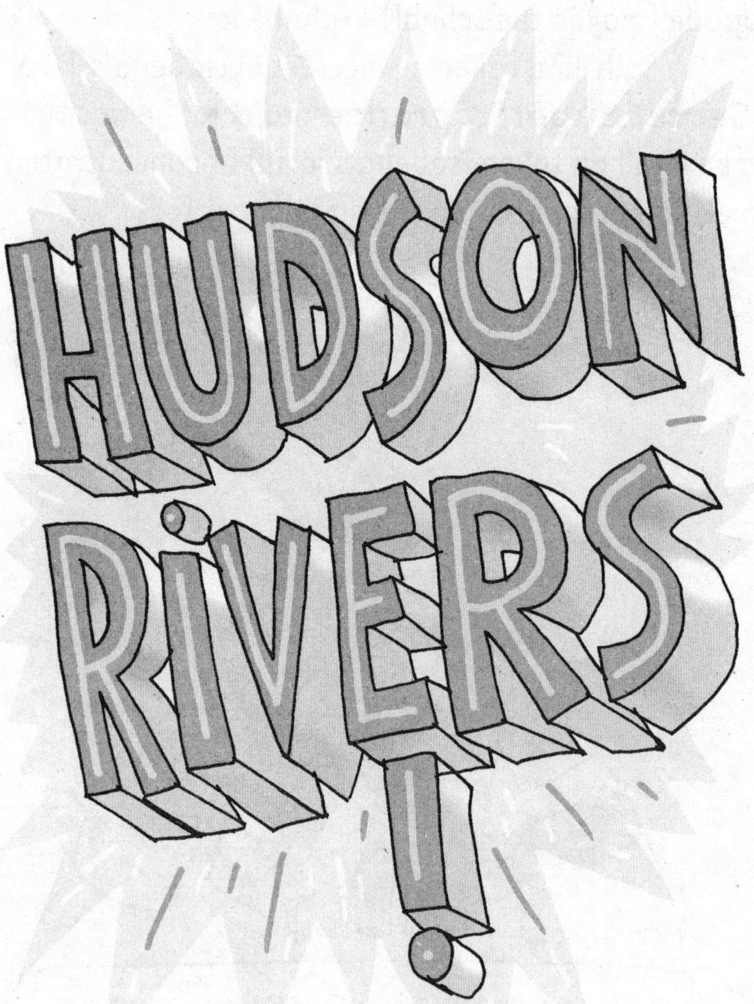
HUDSON RIVERS!

Sally had a crush on him. She had been convinced by discussions with Isabella that Isabella's theory of **Unseen Levels of Popularity** was right. Based on that hypothesis, Sally believed that she had to make room in the middle if she was ever going to be on the same level as Hudson.

EVIL GENIUSES LIKE SALLY ARE AFTER WORLD DOMINATION OR GUYS

So Sally used Isabella's powerful perfume concoction on Margaret by sneaking some into Margaret's backpack when she had gone over to her house to study. The **SuperFragrance** was so totally incredibly complex and enticing that it actually increased Margaret's Popularity, even after she abandoned the other makeover stuff and became the shower drain creature again.

That increase in Margaret's Popularity subsequently lowered Isabella's and mine.

Then all Sally, evil homely genius, had to do was make sure that Isabella and Margaret did their homework wrong and hope that Hudson would wind up with her after one of Mrs. Palmer's predictable partner switches. And he did!

At that point, Sally started using the SuperFragrance on herself, thereby hypnotizing Hudson with the fragrance, which I had found so soothing that I let Margaret eat my pencil.

I was **not** amazed to learn how smart Sally is

I was amazed to learn that smartness is good for something

And she would have gotten away with it, too, if Isabella's sinuses hadn't cleared up. Isabella smelled the distinctive SuperFragrance as she passed Sally's desk. Right after class, Isabella jumped (Isabella said, "leaped like a cat," but I've seen her play volleyball. Trust me: I was being charitable when I said "jumped.") and snatched the jar out of Sally's backpack.

They fought over it, it fell and broke open, and Mrs. Palmer, overcome by the fumes, tripped the alarm, thinking it was some sort of chemical accident. (This would have been worth seeing. Like all girls from big families, Isabella is good at fighting. One time, when one of her big brothers was picking on her, Isabella slapped him so hard that he couldn't taste anything for three weeks. Sally never had a chance.)

It was a total Scooby-Doo moment. Except for the fact that my dog is sort of a reject, and we can't put Sally in jail. But we *are* meddling kids. You have to give us that.

Yup, it all felt pretty good until Hudson walked up and swept Sally away. She shot a glance back at us as if to say, "So what? I *still* got my way, and you're still on the bottom." And she was right. The entire Universe was still just plain wrong.

Behold the Scent of Evil

POOR DUMB HUDSON ↙

Which smells pretty good actually

And then, **IT happened.** I looked up and I saw Angeline coming out of the school. She had been changing in the bathroom when the fire alarm went off. Everybody in the school was outside. And when she opened the door, they all looked. It was the grandest entrance ever made, even though technically, it was an exit.

Angeline was wearing the Bellazure Jeans. But she was walking (I don't know how she does this) in slow motion. Even her hair was blowing in slow motion. Every eye in the school was glued on Angeline and the jeans and the knees of the jeans, which had holes in them.

← This is Beagle's work!

Stinker! These weren't Mom's perfect round bleach holes; these were the irregular holes gnawed by a mean little dog: rough, scraggly, thready holes. **WHY, STINKER? WHY?**

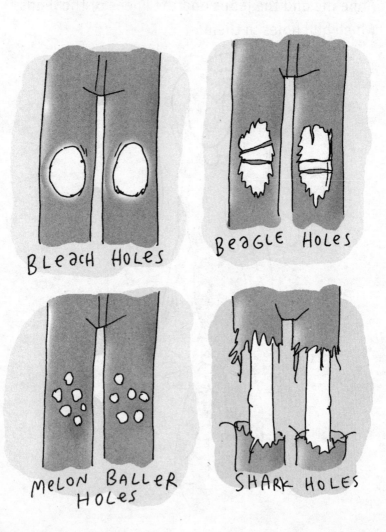

BLEACH HOLES

BEAGLE HOLES

MELON BALLER HOLES

SHARK HOLES

Suddenly, I understood why. It was clear to me that it was because I told Stinker he was twenty pounds overweight. In dog weight, that's **140 POUNDS.** No wonder he was angry. Nobody wants to be told that they are 140 pounds overweight. The jeans were ruined.

But then I saw — we all saw — Angeline's kneecaps peeking out through the openings. It turns out that her knees look more like little tiny perfect bald angel heads than knees.

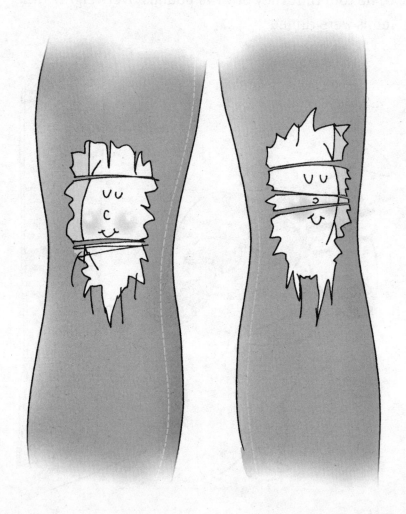

Angeline had just set a trend. Or maybe Stinker had. Either way, fragrance suddenly meant nothing to anyone. We all knew that how people smelled didn't matter, as long as they had jeans like Angeline's.

Angeline had regained her rightful position among the Mega-Populars. And Isabella said that it was like the spell of Margaret's makeover, the SuperFragrance, and the haunted pants had been broken.

Angeline walked over and handed me the money for the jeans. "I'll take 'em," she said.

And then Chip, King of Guys, and Hudson (who had abandoned Sally somewhere) walked up next to Angeline.

"Cool pants," Chip said.

Angeline looked right at me. A lot of things could have happened at that moment. She could have said almost anything.

What she did say was, "Thanks," pointing at Isabella and me. "These two designed 'em."

small feminine heart attacks

Friday 27

Dear Dumb Diary,

Science class was, well, quiet today. Half the kids had on torn jeans, except for Mike Pinsetti, who had torn the elbows out of his sweatshirt. (Not a bad try, for him.)

Isabella was more at peace than I've seen her in weeks. The pants had not been haunted, and the Universe seemed to be in balance again. The true Popularity Order had been restored. Also, Isabella

took some delight in pointing out that now it was absolutely clear that the pants themselves had not **Cut One** in front of Hudson.

It was me. (I blame Mom's cooking.)

Margaret was just happily enjoying pencil after pencil.

Sally didn't look quite so smart anymore, but Isabella and I decided to keep this to ourselves. Isabella says that we had a massive Popularity boost that brought us back up to normal, and maybe even slightly higher, thanks to Angeline. Besides, Sally was just after what we're all after.

Except for Angeline, who already has it.

Anyway, thanks for listening, Dumb Diary. I gotta go. I just remembered there's somebody I owe four hot dogs.

Jamie Kelly

Think you can handle another Jamie Kelly diary? Then check out

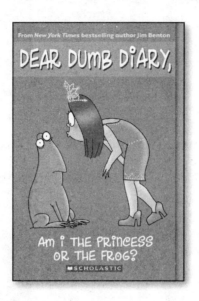

Dear Dumb Diary,

I got another poem today from **You-Know-Who**...

> *She is the fairest blossom, true,*
> *She blooms in any weather.*
> *But I must love her from afar.*
> *We'll never be together.*
>
> *Signed, M. P.*

Can you believe the pain he's in? His suffering? The crushing heartache he endures every time he sees me? Gosh, it just makes me so happy!

Can't get enough of Jamie Kelly?
Check out her other Dear Dumb Diary books!

#1 LET'S PRETEND
THIS NEVER HAPPENED

#2 MY PANTS
ARE HAUNTED!

#3 AM I THE PRINCESS
OR THE FROG?

#4 NEVER DO
ANYTHING, EVER

#5 CAN ADULTS
BECOME HUMAN?

#6 THE PROBLEM
WITH HERE IS THAT IT'S
WHERE I'M FROM

#7 NEVER
UNDERESTIMATE
YOUR DUMBNESS

#8 IT'S NOT MY FAULT
I KNOW EVERYTHING

OUR DUMB DIARY:
A JOURNAL TO SHARE

www.scholastic.com/deardumbdiary